"*Romancing Hollywood Nobody* is a deliciously fun read. Lisa Samson's quirky heroine, Scotty Dawn, had me ROTFLOL on every page. Her satirical tongue rivals Jane Austen's Elizabeth Bennet both in savvy wit and pert opinions. A stylish blogging teen with brains and beauty. What's not to love?—I'm just sayin'!"

—M. C. PEARSON, director, Fiction in Rather Short Takes (FIRST) Blog Alliances

"One of the most powerful voices in Christian fiction."

—PUBLISHERS WEEKLY, review, *Publishers Weekly*

lisa samson

Romancing Hollywood Nobody

Book 3

a novel

For a free catalog
of NavPress books & Bible studies call
1-800-366-7788 (USA) or 1-800-839-4769 (Canada).

www.NavPress.com

THINK
P.O. Box 35001
Colorado Springs, Colorado 80935

ISBN-10: 1-60006-221-0
ISBN-13: 978-1-60006-221-6

Cover design by The DesignWorks Group, David Uttley, www.thedesignworksgroup.com
Cover image by Steve Gardner, www.shootpw.com
Creative Team: Erin Healy, Darla Hightower, Arvid Wallen, Kathy Guist

Published in association with the literary agency of Alive Communications, Inc., 7680 Goddard Street, Suite 200, Colorado Springs, CO 80920 (www.alivecommunications.com).

Library of Congress Cataloging-in-Publication Data

Samson, Lisa, 1964-
Romancing Hollywood nobody. Book 3 / Lisa Samson.
p. cm.
ISBN-13: 978-1-60006-221-6
ISBN-10: 1-60006-221-0
1. Teenage girls--Fiction. 2. Parent and child--Fiction. 3. Domestic fiction. I. Title.
PS3569.A46673R66 2008
813'.54--dc22

2007051983

Printed in the United States of America

1 2 3 4 5 6 7 8 9 10 / 12 11 10 09 08

Other Young Adult Books by Lisa Samson

Finding Hollywood Nobody
Hollywood Nobody
Apples of Gold: A Parable of Purity

Dedication

For Erin B. MARIE Hagerty
Proud to share a name
with one of my all-time
favorite people! Ever.
Love, Aunt Bee

Acknowledgments

Thanks to everyone at Nav, Erin Healy of course, and to all my family and friends, especially those eighteen and under!

Monday, April 30, 6:00 a.m.

My eyes open. Yes, yes, yes. The greatest man in the entire world is brewing coffee right here in the TrailMama.

"Dad."

"Morning, Scotty. The big day."

"Yep."

"And this time, you won't have to drive."

I throw back the covers on my loft bed and slip down to the dinette of our RV. My dad sleeps on the dinette bed. He's usually got it turned back into our kitchen table by 5:00 a.m. What can I say? The guy may be just as much in love with cheese as I am, but honestly? Our body clocks are about as different as Liam Neeson and Seth Green.

You know what I mean?

And we have lots of differences.

For one, he's totally a nonfiction person and I'm fiction all the way. For two, he has no fashion sense whatsoever. And for three, he has way more hope for people at the outset than I do. Man, do I have a lot to learn on that front.

He hands me a mug and I sip the dark liquid. I was roasting coffee beans for a while there, but Dad took the mantle upon himself and he does a better job.

Starbucks Schmarbucks.

He hands me another mug and I head to the back of the TrailMama to wake up Charley. My grandmother looks so sweet in the morning, her frosted, silver-blonde hair fanned out on the pillow. You know, she could pass for an aging mermaid. A really short one, true.

I wave the mug as close as I can to her nose without fear of her rearing up, knocking the mug and burning her face. "Charley . . ." I singsong. "Time to get a move on. Time to get back on the road."

And boy is this a switch!

All I can say is, your life can be going one way for years and years and then, snap-snap-snap-in-a-Z, it looks like it had major plastic surgery.

Only in reverse. Imagine life just getting more and more real. I like it.

Charley opens her eyes. "Hey, baby. You brought me coffee. You get groovier every day."

She's a hippie. What can I say?

And she started drinking coffee again when I ran away last fall in Texas. I mean, I didn't *really* run away. I went somewhere with a perfectly good reason for not telling anyone, and I was planning to return as soon as my mission was done.

She scootches up to a sitting position, hair still in a cloud, takes the mug and, with that dazzling smile still on her face (think Kate Hudson) sips the coffee. She sighs.

"I know," I say. "How did we make it so long without him?"

"Now that he's with us, I don't know. But somehow we did, didn't we, baby? It may not have always been graceful and smooth, but we made it together."

I rub her shoulder. "Yeah. I guess you could say we pretty much did."

The engine hums its movin'-on song. "Dad's ready to pull out. Let's hit it."

"Scotland, here we come."

Scotland? Well, sort of.

An hour later

This has been a great school year. In addition to the online courses I'm taking through Indiana University High School, Dad's been teaching me and man, is he smart. I'm sure most sixteen-(almost seventeen)-year-olds think their fathers are the smartest guys in the world, but in my case it happens to be true.

Okay, even I have to admit he probably won't win the Nobel Prize for physics or anything, but he's street smart and there's no replacing that sort of thing. Big plus: he knows high school math. We're both living under the radar. And he's taken our faux last name. Dawn. He's now Ezra Fitzgerald Dawn. After Ezra Pound, one of F. Scott Fitzgerald's Lost Generation friends.

I'm just lovin' that.

"Your mom would have loved the name change, Scotty."

He told me about his life as an FBI agent, some of the cases he worked on, and well, I'd like to tell you he had a life like Sydney Bristow's in *Alias*, but he probably spent most of his time on computer work and sitting around on his butt waiting for someone to make a move. The FBI, apparently, prefers to trick people more than corner them in showdowns and shootouts. The Robertsman case was his first time undercover in the field and we know how terribly that worked out for him. And me. And Charley. And Babette, my mother.

I pull out my math book and sit in the passenger seat of the TrailMama. "Ready for some 'rithmetic, Dad?"

"You bet." He turns to me and smiles. His smile still makes my heart warm up like a griddle ready to make smiley-face pancakes. I flip on my book light.

It's still dark and we're headed to Asheville, North Carolina for Charley's latest shoot. A film about Bonnie Prince Charlie called *Charlie's Lament.* How ironic is that? The director, Bartholomew (don't dare call him Bart) Evans, is a real jerk. I'm not going to be hanging around the set much even though Liam Neeson is Lord George Murray, the voice of reason Prince Charlie refused to listen to. But hey, that's my history lesson. We're still on math.

I finish up the last lesson in geometry . . . finally! Honestly, I still don't understand it without a mammoth amount of help, but the workbook's filled and that's a good thing.

There.

I set down my pen. "Finished!"

Dad gives a nod as he continues to look out the windshield. You might guess, despite the tattoos, piercings, and his gleaming bald head, he's a very careful driver. And he won't let me drive like Charley did.

"So . . . driver's license then, right?"

He's been holding that over my head so I'd finish the math course.

"You know it. After the film, we'll request your new birth certificate and go from there."

"What state are we supposedly from?" The FBI has given us a new identity, official papers and all that.

"Wyoming."

"Are you kidding me? Wyoming? Why?"

"Think about it, honey. Who's from Wyoming?"

"Lots of people?"

"Know any of them?"

"Uh. No."

"See?"

"Okay, Wyoming it is, then."

"You realize you'll only have my beat-up old black truck to drive around." The same truck we're towing behind the TrailMama.

"I'll take it."

So here's the thing. The rest of the entire world thinks my father was shot in the chest and killed when he was outed by a branch of the mob he was after. This mob was financing James Robertsman's campaign for governor of Maryland.

The guy's running for president of the United States now.

I kid you not.

Wish I was kidding.

We thought he was after us for several years because Charley knew too much. But then last fall, we found out the guy chasing me was my father, and Robertsman is most likely cocky enough to think he took care of everything he needed. I say that's quite all right. Although, I have to admit, the fact that a dirtbag like that guy may end up in the Oval Office sickens me to no end.

Thanks to that guy, we had been running in fear from my own father.

The thing is, I could be really mad about all those wasted years, and a portion of me feels that way. But we've been given another chance, and I'll be darned if I throw away these days being angry. There's too much to be thankful for.

Don't get me wrong. I still have my surly days. I don't want Dad and Charley to think they have it as easy as all that!

Okay, time to blog.

Hollywood Nobody: April 30

Let's cut to the chase, Nobodies!

Today's Seth News: It's official. Seth Haas and Karissa Bonano are officially each other's exclusive main squeeze. The two were seen coming out of a popular LA tattoo parlor with each other's names on the inside of their forearms. How cliché. And pass the barf bag.

Today's Violette Dillinger Report: Violette has broken up with Joe Mason of Sweet Margaret. She wanted you all to know that long-distance romances are hard for any couple, but especially for people as young as she is. "Joe needed to live his life. I'm on the road a lot. It wasn't fair to either of us." Sounds like she's definitely not on the road to Britney. I'm just sayin'.

Today's Rave: Mandy Moore. The girl can really sing! And her latest album is filled with good songs. The bubble gum days of insipid teen heartbreak are over. She's finally come into her own. (Wish some others would follow her example, but I won't hold my breath. And man, are we on the theme of bratty stars today or what? Well, there are just so many of them from which to choose!)

Today's Rant: Crazy expensive celebrity weddings. What? If they spend more, will they be more likely to stay together? I have no idea. Mariah Carey's $25,000 dress pales in comparison to Catherine Zeta-Jones's $100,000 gown. What are those things made of?

Today's Quote: "Dream as if you'll live forever, live as if you'll die today." James Dean

Well, if that's the case, Mr. Dean, pass the guacamole Doritos and let's forget about college!

Later!

Later

Text message from Seth. Oh brother.

Seth: Hey Sctty.
Me: Hey, Mr. New Tattoo.
Seth: U saw?
Me: All over the tabloids.
Seth: Yeah.
Me: So you're going to marry her?
Seth: I dnt knw.

Oh sheesh.

Me: Tattoo removal is quite painful I hear.
Seth: Where r u?
Me: On our way to NC and another shoot. Scottish romance.
Seth: Cool. Im filmng in Nrth Dkota tomrw.
Me: Karissa joining you?
Seth: Yes. Shes btwn flms.
Me: Of course she is.
Seth: Sctty, my moms cancer is bck.

Crap! Why was I being so mean? It always bites me in the behind when I'm mean.

Me: Oh my gosh, Seth. I'm so sorry.

I call him and he picks up right away.

"What happened?"

"She had her yearly checkup and it was back."

"Is it bad?"

"She starts chemo right away."

"I'm really sorry, Seth. You can't know how much."

"No, I think I do. You know what it's like to lose your mother."

"She's not going to die."

"I hope you're right."

"When did you find out?"

"Last week. I knew you'd at least pray for her. And Dad too."

"And you."

"Yeah. I guess."

What we both don't say is that Karissa won't pray. She'd probably laugh at Seth for even asking. But I'm not going to go there. Even I know that would be over the line.

"Hey, I gotta go," he says. "I've got a lot of packing to do before I catch my flight."

"Okay. Keep me posted, Seth."

"I will."

He's silent for a moment. Then, "Scotty?"

"Yeah?"

"I know I'm not the greatest friend in the world. I know I

dissed you in Marshall and I wanted to apologize."

"Apology accepted."

Notice I didn't say, "That's okay." Because it wasn't okay. And it still isn't. But I forgive him. Seth is my brother figure. I only get so mad at him because I don't want him to do things he'll regret. And he's going to regret Karissa. Oh man, someday he's going to wish he never laid eyes on that girl.

And honestly? I'm still crushing on him a little bit. He's too old for me, yeah, I get it.

I set down my phone on the dashboard. "Wow."

"What is it?" Charley asks from where she sits at the dinette looking at my computer for old-time food from Scotland. I hate to tell her, but it's going to be a lot of meat, and with her being a vegan and all, oh my gosh. It's not going to be a good shoot.

"Seth's mom's cancer has returned."

"Oh no." Dad.

"Is Seth upset?" Charley. "Never mind. Of course he is."

"I dunno. He went and got tattoos with Karissa the day before yesterday."

Dad shakes his head. "That doesn't mean he isn't hurting, honey. The fact that he did something so permanent could be construed that he's hurting a great deal."

"It's true." Charley.

Maybe I need to learn to give Seth the benefit of the doubt. I text him again.

> Me: Can I have your mom's address? I want to send her a card.

But I don't hear back. He's probably on his way to the airport, picking up the Karissa along the way in his new convertible Volvo. It's a beauty. Too bad the beast will be sitting in the passenger seat.

Noon

Well, the moratorium on cheese has been lifted! Charley has relegated all those decisions to Dad and thank goodness for that. We're sitting in an Arby's in Petersburg, Virginia. Dad's eating a bacon cheddar roast beef, and I've got a double order of mozzarella sticks. Charley's in the camper eating beans and brown rice. "Don't ask me to witness the carnage," she said.

Dad laughed and gave her a hug. Charley needs more hugs than just I can give her, and Dad's happy to provide. He's a very huggy person. I can totally see why my mother fell for him. And the pictures of him as a young man? Totally a hottie. He was thin back then, and the hair that's now nonexistent (yes, he shaves his head, but still) was clipped short, allowing his dark curls to frame his brow. It's amazing what fourteen years will do to a person, but honestly, I don't care. He's my Dad. And his smile is still the greatest thing. You just can't change that. Besides, he's still got his good teeth. He took us all to the dentist this winter and man, did I have some cavities despite the fact that Charley limited my sugar intake. Sometimes you just can't fight genetics.

He pulls out a blue spiral-bound notebook and takes a sip of coffee. "Okay, we've checked out all the morgue records east of the Mississippi. Nothing matching Babette."

So there's hope, maybe?

"And you really don't think they would have done anything farther west?"

"No, honey. They stick to their territory. I was particularly worried about the East Coast. But nothing."

I inhale deeply. "So what's next?"

"Well, I talked with the agent who's on it all right now."

"They're still working on Robertsman?"

"Of course. He's slippery. So slippery that everybody knows that someday he's going to slip up. It's our greatest hope with this sort of thing."

I pick up a mozzarella stick. "Can they get him on income-tax evasion or something?"

He laughs. "Oh, Scotty. I think he's smarter than Al Capone was."

"True. So what did the agent say?"

"He hasn't heard a thing concerning your mom, but he did give me a list of Robertsman's favorite hangouts." He raises one brow.

"No, Dad. I know what you're thinking. It's too dangerous."

"Perhaps."

Now, if you could see what my dad really looks like, his choice of the word "perhaps" is comical. He should be saying, "No kidding," or, "Yeah, yeah, yeah."

I bite down on my stick. He bites into his sandwich.

You see, here's the thing. We talk about this, and it's serious stuff, don't get me wrong. But it's our life. We talk about serious things over food, on the road, wherever we are. And it isn't callous, and it doesn't make these matters less important. It's just part of who we are.

"So you're going to hang out around these places?"

"On the weekends."

"Of course."

"I do have my day job and you to consider."

"I know, Dad. It was your MO finding me."

"Exactly."

"How will you get there?"

"I'll fly back and forth. Rent a car."

I sip my water. "Isn't that expensive?"

"Yes. But I've saved up enough over the years."

We sit in silence for a while, chewing on our food and our thoughts.

"So what are some of the places?"

"Well, there's a restaurant in Little Italy."

"Figures."

"I know. But there you have it. The main one is called Mama Agnese's."

"Agnes? Doesn't that mean *holy*?"

"Uh-huh. Ironic, isn't it?"

I smash the cheese-stick box. "Remember that scene in *The Godfather* where people are out doing a hit and Al Pacino is in church promising to defend the faith and live a holy life for the child who's being baptized as his godchild?"

"What are you doing watching that movie at your age?"

"Oh, please, Dad. Think about it. I was living with Charley. I could've gotten away with a whole lot more."

"I understand it. I don't have to like it, honey."

"True. Anyway, how do people go to church and all, make holy promises before God, and then just go about the evil business?"

He shakes his head. "I don't know. Robertsman is the same,

Scotty. Never misses a Sunday at his church."

I rest my chin in my palm. "I don't get it."

"Me either."

"Will you be careful?"

"I'm trained in this sort of thing."

"Yeah, and look where it got you last time."

"Hey, I'm alive aren't I?"

Okay, there is that, I suppose.

"Are you going to tell Charley what you're doing?"

"Yes. She deserves to know."

"She'll worry like crazy."

"Of course she will. Mothers deserve to worry about their children."

I consider that. He's right. "Do you think, if Mom is still alive, that she worries about me?"

"Oh, I'd say you can count on that."

"Dad? What if she's not alive? What do we do then?"

He shakes his head. "It'll take a while to get over it. But we'll be together, Scotty. We'll do what we have to do."

It's true.

Man, I can't get over how much my life has changed in just one year.

"Ready to hit the road?" he asks.

"Let's go."

Five o'clock

The landscape is breathtaking. I know that sounds cliché, but honestly, I've sucked in my breath at least a dozen times since we've entered the Great Smoky Mountains. Amazing. Even Charley had to look up from her planning and stare out the picture window by the dinette.

"Do you have the address for the campground?" I ask.

"Yes." She flips to the front of her notebook. As flighty as she can seem—and yes, she's sitting there in a caftan of bright orange, gold, and hot-pink paisley with her silver-blonde hair in two braids—she keeps detailed notes for each shoot. Each shoot gets a separate binder. This one is lime green.

She shoots off the address and I Google Map it. We're only fifteen minutes away. Yes!

I hop on the Fireside Campground website. Right in the mountains. The scenery is far-reaching and well, yes, breathtaking. "It does sort of look like Scotland."

"It's why a lot of Scots settled in the area," Dad says from the driver's seat.

"So, who's starring in it besides Liam Neeson?" I ask. Love the guy.

Charley's eyes light up, and her eyes never light up during conversations about actors. In her line of work, they're mostly a necessary evil, even though she's too nice to admit it out loud. "Anthony Harris."

"Whoa." Dad.

"Are you kidding me?"

"Why would I kid about that?" she asks.

"Charley, it's a figure of speech. I know you're not really kidding. It's like saying, 'No way!' or 'I can't believe it!'"

Sometimes you just have to explain these things.

"I love that guy!" Dad.

"Me too, Dad. He was the best John Barclay ever."

The Barclay spy series took a back seat to James Bond, but shouldn't have. The movies never made it "across the pond" in a big way.

"I think so too." Charley. "But his performance in *Golden Years* stole my breath away."

One of those cancer stories where the old man sees what a wreck he made of his life and seeks to make amends before he dies. Yes, it was breathtaking too.

"That Scottish accent of his is hard to turn your back on," I say.

"Tell me about it." Charley flips her binder back to her shopping-list page.

"Well, okay. You see the way that they pronounce their *r*'s at the back of their throat—"

"Figure of speech, Scotty."

I laugh. "I know. Just kidding, Charley, just kidding."

10:00 p.m.

I'm sitting outside the TrailMama in my pink soccer-mom chair, bundled up in a blanket, looking up into the mass of stars. I should be reading my book for English, but I'm enjoying the darkness, a velvety darkness, and the slight wind in the trees.

Cell phone beeps. Seth texts me his mom's address.

Me: Got it. Thanks. You okay?

Seth: Yeah. Were at th hotl in fargo. Stll cld here

Me: We're at the shoot in NC. Chilly here, but breathtaking.

Seth: Gtta go. Erly cll tmorrw

Me: See ya.

Seth: Bye

I call Grammie and Grampie.

"Hello, dear!" Grammie says.

"We're here safe and sound."

"Lovely."

"Have you guys left OC yet?"

"No. We've decided to stay in Maryland and look around at real estate."

"Really? Like, a real house?"

She laughs. "Yes, Scotty. Grampie and I are thinking we should have a home base for all of us."

"At the beach?!" I practically scream.

"So you approve?"

"Most definitely. Will you still go out on the road in the Beaver Marquis?" The greatest motor home ever.

"Oh, my. You can't remove the wanderlust from us. And George still needs to write his travel articles."

Grammie is the greatest woman. She has a cloud of silver hair that she sometimes wears in turbans. And she wears cool jewelry you won't find at the mall. And Grampie? He's this classy, preppy-looking man with his own mane of silver hair. Why my dad is so bald is beyond me. Yeah, he shaves, but there's a reason for that. It's pretty darn thin up top.

But I still think he's perfect.

"Get Grampie to e-mail me with the listings."

"Oh, we wouldn't dream of buying something you didn't approve of first." She laughs.

"I hope not. I mean, I'm going to be the one around there getting the tan and working summers and all that stuff."

"We can think of nothing better than having you stay with us during breaks."

And summer is coming soon!

Tuesday, May 1, 8:00 a.m.

Oh my goodness, what is that noise?

I lift my head off the pillow. Dad looks up at me from his computer and laughs.

"Bagpipes," he says.

"Whoa."

"You'll get used to the sound. You might even like it."

"Sounds like something's dying out there."

He stands up and pours me some coffee. "Let's take a walk and see things. I've never really been around a movie set before."

"A lot of almosts during the days you were looking for me, though."

"You know it."

I jump down from my loft and hug him.

"Okay, let me get dressed and we'll head on out."

What to wear, what to wear? Because, let's face it, bagpipes may sound a little scary, but the guys playing them in those fabulous kilts? I'm just sayin'.

It's still chilly so I throw on a pair of black corduroy pants and Charley's old fisherman's sweater from Ireland and a pair of black leather clogs. I scrape my curly hair back in a classy, tight bun. With a pair of Audrey Hepburn sunglasses, I have to admit, I'm not shabby. "Ready, Dad?"

"Wow, honey. You sure you want to be seen with this old scruffer?"

"Are you kidding me?"

So we head out, arm in arm. It's so great not having to camp on the outskirts anymore, knowing nobody's chasing us. We're the only people staying on site in our own camper. When my grandmother works for Jeremy Winger, our favorite director, he stays nearby in his vintage Airstream camper. I miss Jeremy.

"Now watch out for Bartholomew Evans, the director," I tell Dad.

"Why?"

"He's horrible. Treats people like, well, like they're not people at all. But he gets the job done, I guess. I mean, if people are willing to subjugate themselves to a mess like that, I suppose they get what they deserve."

Dad shakes his head. "No, Scotty. He's wrong to treat people like that. Period."

"Yeah. I guess it's easy to let big-time directors off the hook."

"Don't do it."

"Believe me. It's not a stretch for me! I rarely let people off the hook."

"Well don't start."

I wrinkle my nose at him. "Okay, boss."

We stroll by the stars' trailers. Shooting actually begins tomorrow. Charley's going to be doing her shopping today, but right now she's setting up her kitchen trailer.

Dad and I step up inside when we get to it.

"Hey, you two!"

I kiss Charley's cheek. "You nervous?"

She nods and opens a drawer to inspect her utensils. "My first major motion picture. I hope I can do it."

"Lots of meat," I remind her.

Satisfied with the contents of the drawer, she slides it shut. "Oh, baby, I know! I know!"

"You'll do fine," Dad says. "You've done this all a million times, right?"

"Well, maybe not a million. Is it okay if I use your truck to shop today, Ezra?"

Ezra. It still cracks me up the way we're all going by fake names out in public.

"Of course."

We head back out a couple of minutes later. The bagpipes are still playing and I see a pipe band across the field. They're all dressed in regular clothing, jeans and jackets.

"Let's go watch!"

"Okay," Dad says.

The grass, still covered with dew, soaks our shoes. We stand at the edge of the clearing. The pipe band marches around playing a Scottish tune one hears pipe bands play—if they so happen to hear a pipe band play.

"What's that song, Dad?"

"'Scotland the Brave.'"

"I like it."

"Me too."

"Do you think it was written before 1745?"

"Probably not."

I shrug. "They'll use it anyway, though."

He laughs. "You're so cynical about Hollywood, honey."

"And my cynicism is well deserved."

"Granted."

The band approaches us, marching in single file. An older man with pipes leads the way. The pipers follow and then the drummers. The third piper in is young! I'll bet he's only a little older than I am.

And boy is he cute! Solidly built, but not at all overweight. I'll bet he's got those powerful soccer-player calves. Wavy, dirty-blond hair on the longish side. And even as he passes by, I see eyes so blue they blend with the sky overhead.

One of them winks at me.

And his eyes smile, even though his mouth, blowing air into the plaid bag underneath his arm, cannot. His cheeks are puffed out like Dizzy Gillespie's when he's blowing on his trumpet.

I'm in such shock, he passes me by before I can react.

"I saw that, Scotty."

"He was pretty cute."

"I'd think so if I was a teenage girl."

We laugh.

"Hey, remove yourselves from my field!" somebody yells.

We turn and there he is, the infamous Bartholomew Evans.

"Oh, man." I tug on Dad's arm.

But Dad walks right toward the man. "Is there some sort of problem?"

"No unauthorized personnel are allowed on this set."

Dad pulls out a badge. He still has his old badge? How in the world did he get away with that? Or is there something I don't know? "Is there a problem?"

Bartholomew turns white. "I guess not. Just stay out of the way."

"Are we in the way right now?" Dad asks. "Are you filming right now?"

"No."

"Then we'll listen to the band."

"Who's the girl?"

"She's the granddaughter of the food stylist, and she's my daughter. She's been around sets all her life."

"Well, isn't that just dandy?" Bart sneers.

Okay, so some description of this guy here. Bartholomew Evans is Mr. Artsy Fartsy. Now our friend Jeremy is the comfy cowboy-booted type of guy. Mr. Artsy Fartsy wears all black all the time, and how original. He pulls his dark-brown hair back into a ponytail, which reaches just below his shoulders and I swear, he probably acts all Fabio when he's by himself and looking in one of his, oh, say, eight thousand mirrors. He wears Italian loafers and a scarf, usually in some dull color like brown or dirty gold or something.

"Yes. It certainly is. Now so you know, because of my daughter's knowledge of film sets, we'll know when to make ourselves scarce."

Go, Dad.

"All right?" he says. But he's not really asking.

Evans turns around.

Dad and I hold our hands over our mouths and laugh.

"We'll have to make sure to keep clear of him," he says. "That guy is no fun."

"What a downer! Hey, can we ride into town? I want to get a card for Seth's mom."

"You got it."

Thirty minutes later

Charley drops us off on Wall Street. Yeah, Wall Street. A place with funky shops that sell beads and pottery and the like. We head into a small gift shop, and I make for the rack of cards in the back corner. A TV plays by the register counter.

Great. Some Hollywood news-type show. But hey, it'll be good for the blog. I cross my arms across my abdomen and watch the usual display of movie news and one heartbreaking story of underage drinking.

And there he is. Right in the middle of a gang of young stars.

Seth.

He's smiling in a way that says, "I'm so hot nobody can touch me." His arm is around Karissa, and the voice-over is calling the group the Splat Pack. Presumably because they're always so plastered.

Great. Just great.

Dad sidles up.

"See?" I point to the screen. "I warned him she'd take him places he shouldn't go. How do they not get arrested? Who lets them into these clubs?"

Dad shrugs. "You're the one who knows about Hollywood, not me."

"No, Dad. I don't really know it. I'm not even close to being an insider. I guess money talks."

"You got that right, honey."

I pay for a cute card, blank inside, with a flower fairy on the outside. Call me goomy, but I love flower fairies.

We sit outside on a bench with two cups of fresh coffee, and I write out the card, trying to express my dismay without discouraging her, yet trying to offer hope and encouragement. Man, this is hard. Dad returns calls for work on his cell phone.

I text Seth after I'm finished.

Me: The Splat Pack?

He doesn't text back. Figures.

Three hours later

Everything's abuzz back at camp. An older bagpiper who's sitting at the canteen drinking an iced tea tells me Anthony Harris has arrived.

Oh joy!

You just have to love everything about Anthony Harris. And

I hear he's a real gem to work with, highly professional, not given to prima donnaism. He doesn't even like having his own trailer, preferring just to sit on the sidelines and watch what's going on. He brings his own folding chair. It's his "Good Luck Chair."

So cool.

He's in conversation with Mr. Artsy. Oh, well. We'll be here for a while. Maybe I can get a chance to talk with him eventually.

"Hey, I've got to get back to work," Dad whispers. "I'll be at the RV. You okay to wander around by yourself?"

"I'm almost seventeen, Dad."

"There you go then. If you see Charley, tell her I'll make dinner. Ask her what time."

"You got it." I love the mundane details of being in a family, things like dinnertimes and even laundry. Speaking of which, I've got to get our dirty clothes together and get over to the campground's Laundromat.

Thirty minutes later

It smells kinda funky in here. Moist and cementy. The machines are probably twice as old as I am, but they're clean. I stuff the whites in one machine, the darks in another, and the lights in a third. Soon the machines are filled and the agitation begins.

I love the sound of washing machines. Is that crazy or what?

I pull out my computer and my heart is sore. You know, it was one thing writing about Seth when he was doing stupid Karissa things. But now that he's doing really stupid alcohol-drunken-mess things, I'm sad. Karissa makes me jealous. Him being part of the Splat Pack makes me mourn.

I can't write about it on Hollywood Nobody. Seth's mom, Edie, reads my blog. (Seth doesn't even know I'm Hollywood Nobody!) And she just doesn't need to know about this right now. She's got enough worries as it is.

So I pull out Elaine, my diary. Yeah, yeah, yeah. A diary. How cliché. But I don't have any friends my age. Except for Grace, who lives in Texas and can only talk on the phone every so often because she's seventeen and a mom these days and thank you, God, I've been spared from that sort of mess.

Dear Elaine,

I'm tired of my blog. You know all this stuff is funny and sassy and interesting when you're dealing with somebody you don't know. But right now, I don't think I can post a thing. Because all of these people, as stupid as they can be at times and as frustrating and mean and self-centered, well, somebody knows them too.

Why is Seth acting like this? I really thought maybe he'd be different, be one of the people who could withstand the pressures of his job and the people he finds himself with. I really did.

It's just so sad.

I shut the diary. Now, I'm not a crier. But I could cry right now if I let myself. Instead, I pray. Not some self-righteous prayer of a person who does the right thing at the right time, but more of a pleading sort of thing: for Seth, his mom, their entire family. Because when troubles begin, they seem to rain down like crazy. Oh Jesus, keep Seth from doing something really, really stupid.

Ten minutes later

Okay, I'm about as able to concentrate on prayer as celebrities are able to concentrate on anything other than themselves.

Man, I'm in a crazy mood.

A door in the back of the Laundromat opens, and someone with two big bags of laundry enters the room.

He drops the bags in front of the two remaining machines.

It's the young bagpiper and be still my beating heart.

Before he can see me, I hurry out of the building.

Why? I don't know.

Maybe because if he talks to me, I'll say something really stupid.

Six o'clock

"Charley?" I step up into the kitchen trailer.

No answer.

Okay, so supper's waiting. Dad cooked up a vegetable stew

and grilled chicken for me and himself. She was supposed to be back at the TrailMama by now.

Oh well. Must have had something take her by surprise.

I head over to the canteen. Maybe she needed something to drink.

The gray clouds overhead want to burst any minute. It's going to be a nice calm night of reading with rain pattering on the aluminum roof. Maybe I'll feel like blogging. Who knows?

There she is, standing with Mr. Artsy.

She sees me before he does, and she shakes her head ever so slightly at me. I stop by a picnic table and sit down.

"I'm just asking for half a cow roasting over a spit!" Evans screams. Charley flinches.

That waste of a human being!

She murmurs something. Probably that it's going to take some time to order half a cow.

"It needs to be ready for the shoot tomorrow afternoon, Ms. Dawn. If you can't do it, believe me, I'll find somebody who can." He looks over at me. Crap. "And that girl better stay out of my way. I didn't say you could bring your family. It's against union policies anyway."

"We're staying here on our own. We rented the lot our camper is on."

"She'd better keep off the set and stay away from any of the trailers and the equipment."

"She's a good girl, Mr. Evans—"

"I don't care! Now get out of here!"

"But—"

"Now, you flaky idiot! I knew I should've hired somebody else."

She turns away and walks toward me and heaven help us, her foot catches an electrical cord snaking away from the canteen and she falls flat on her face.

"Charley!" I yell, gaining my feet and running toward her.

She starts to climb to her feet.

A man steps up behind me. "Let me help you."

And it's Anthony Harris. He leans down and offers his hand. Charley takes it and stands up. She brushes the grass from her sweater. "Thanks."

Evans walks over. "Harris. I've got some things to go over with you, if you don't mind."

The actor drips an icy stare over the director. "It's after six. I'm off the clock. Sorry. Union rules and all that."

He offers Charley his arm. "Can I escort you back to your caravan, miss?"

Miss. Isn't that cute?

"Oh. I . . . uh, okay."

"And you as well?" He looks at me.

"I'm right behind you."

Dad, of course, invites Harris in to dinner like he's just another guy. I mean, I guess when you've been shot by a mobster and survived, an actor isn't going to intimidate you.

"Thank you. I'm a bit hungry and don't feel like going into town."

So I set an extra plate while Charley freshens up.

Dad introduces himself as he spoons up the stew. He removes the platter of chicken keeping warm in the oven.

When Charley emerges, I feel so proud. She's twirled her hair into a clip, some silvery tendrils framing her gentle face. She wears an Indian-print shirt over some jeans, and long silver turquoise earrings complete it all to perfection. She's so beautiful.

I steal a look at Harris. Yeah, he sees what I see. He invites her to sit next to him in the dinette.

When we sit at the table, Dad says grace and Harris doesn't look like he thinks a thing about it. That's good. I mean, I'm all for prayer, but grace in front of a stranger is a little embarrassing. But his hearty "Amen!" at the end drives away any of that.

"My dad was a minister in Edinburgh," he explains.

Dad passes the chicken his way.

"No thanks, if you don't mind. I'm a vegetarian."

Charley's head snaps up. "Really? I'm vegan."

I roll my eyes at Dad. Great. Just great.

"Well, there's plenty of stew," Dad says. "Eat up."

After the meal, I set up our camp chairs outside, and Dad starts a campfire in the nearby circle of stones. I expect Harris to leave, but instead, he sits down and removes a pipe from his pocket.

I run inside for a blanket and text Seth.

Me: You'll never believe it! Anthony Harris just had dinner in our RV. And he's sitting outside in my pink soccer-mom chair smoking a pipe!

Seth: Crzy!

Me: Where are you?

Seth: At dnnr w Krrsa and some of th cst.

Dinner? Yeah right. He's probably tying one on. Or two. Or three.

Me: Gotta get back out there.
Seth: C ya.

Harris is talking about his life in Scotland. The campfire warms his patrician features. The man really is good-looking. Like a bigger Pierce Brosnan all grown up, with white hair and bigger teeth.

Charley, who's usually in bed by now, is hanging on to his every word, and I don't blame her. That accent is enough to make anybody listen long into the night. And his hands are so beautiful, shapely and masculine, but expressive in their movements.

Well, he is an actor.

With this guy, however, it's easy to forget. What a surprise.

I like it!

His mother died when he was only seventeen and he helped raise his younger siblings, who are all doing quite well now, thank you.

And he's fascinated by our life in the RV.

"Aye, this is living. Going from place to place, no cares, no upkeep on the castle."

I perk up. "That's right. You own a castle, don't you?"

"Aye. I'm a regular prince." And he laughs at his own joke. The laugh is much deeper and boomier in real life. He did Shakespeare as a young man and I can see why.

He turns to Charley. "About that half a cow . . ."

"You heard Mr. Evans?" Charley.

"Unfortunately. He's a bit overboard, isn't he?"

"You said it," I say.

"I don't know what I'm going to do," she says. "I've got to find a phone book and start calling butchers I guess. Or farms. I don't even know."

"Let's go." Harris.

"What?" Charley.

"Let's go into town and have a coffee. I'll ask the owner for their phone book, and we'll set to work."

"It's going to cost a fortune." She shakes her head. "This is awful."

"I'll do the calling. And we'll rest on the fact that there aren't many people who wouldn't butcher a cow in the middle of the night for John Barclay, secret agent."

Charley looks like she's about to cry. "Oh, that poor cow."

Harris stands up, holds out his hand, and she takes it as she rises from the chair. "Shall we, fair lady? We'll ask forgiveness from the poor creature together."

Harris dumps the contents of his pipe into the fire, then he and Charley disappear into the darkness toward the parking lot.

"Go figure." I shake my head.

"I'm with you."

"Not to mention the fact they're both vegetarians."

"Hardly seems fair."

Dad and I laugh and sit back down in front of the fire, only this time, I snuggle in his lap as he circles his arms around me and tells me about the time I busted my forehead on the coffee table.

I love these stories. I love these times.

Wednesday, May 2

Charley's bed hasn't been slept in.

Oh my gosh!

I jump down from my loft, open the TrailMama's door, and the smell of roasting meat hits me.

I look at the clock—7:00 a.m.

"Dad? How long have you been up?"

"Since five. Charley came in and said, 'Mission accomplished.' Harris found a farmer who had just butchered a cow and was glad to sell them half. He even delivered it and set up the spit. Those two have been tending it all night."

"Harris and Charley?"

"Uh-huh."

"Wow. He's a really nice man, isn't he?"

I so love it when people are nice.

"Seems so."

"Figures you'd say that."

"Can't help it. I know what people are capable of. But yes, it would surprise me if that was an act."

"Oh, I know an act!"

I wonder what Jeremy will think of this! Should I tell him? I mean, maybe he should be jealous.

Oh, Scotty, come on! Anthony Harris interested in Charley? I mean, she's great and all, but Anthony Harris? I don't think so. He was just bored last night and needed something to do.

I throw on jeans and a coat, slip into some clogs, and head toward the aroma of roasting beef. There they sit, the two of them in our folding chairs, both wrapped in blankets. Charley's head is slumped to the side, toward Harris, and he's smoking his pipe again, ankle resting on the opposite knee. The smoke curls into the sky along with the smoke from the roasting fire.

"Hey," I say.

"Oh, hello there, Scotty. She fell asleep an hour ago."

"Thanks for doing this."

He waves my gratitude away. "Glad to. I can't abide Evans. Was just interested in the project. Scotland needs a real telling of Bonnie Prince Charlie."

"From what I can ascertain"—I shove my hands in my pockets—"he made some pretty stupid decisions."

"You enjoy history?"

"Yes."

"Your grandmother tells me you're quite the smart one."

I shake my head. "Not really. I just don't have much else to do."

"Good for you, then."

"Can I get you some breakfast? My dad makes the best oatmeal."

"I'd be grateful."

"You could've slept in a warm hotel room."

"This was more interesting. Your grandmother's good company."

"Mr. Harris!" Evans strides our way.

"Gotta go!"

And I run back to the RV before he can yell at me too.

Three hours later

"Dad, do you really think Babette's dead?"

"I do, Scotty. She'd have found me. I'd have found her. We were that kind of couple."

We're sitting at the Laundromat. I forgot to bring the brights yesterday.

"What's it like to be in love like that?"

He closes his laptop. "It's the most wonderful thing in the world."

"Tell me again how you guys met."

"You want to hear it *again*?"

"Are you kidding me? It's the most romantic story ever!"

He sets his computer on the folding table. "Well, okay."

And he tells the tale that's still fresh and young. About how my mother walked away from the food line of the snack shop at Towson State. She walked right out of her sneaker. Just one of them. And she looked down, but the tray was in her hands and she couldn't find an empty table nearby.

He jumped up, retrieved the shoe and ushered her to his table.

"And I knelt down and put the shoe back on her foot."

Like Cinderella and Prince Charming.

Ah. Ain't life beautiful sometimes?

"She looked at me and she saw me, honey. All of me. All in one glance. And we were together from that day on."

They married young. Both sophomores. Set themselves up in a little apartment near campus and he watched while she turned into a beautiful, intelligent woman with a nose for a good story.

They ate Chinese takeout when she was reporting and he was getting his masters in criminology.

"We'd watch a lot of movies. Listen to records. And we just loved each other."

But he looks so sad now. And I'm sorry I asked him.

"I hope she's alive," I say.

"I don't want to hope. If she's not . . ."

Now it's up to me to do the brave talking. But I don't know what to say.

Luckily, the young bagpiper walks into the room. "Hey."

"Hi!" Dad perks right up. "You on your way to the set?"

"Nah. No piping needed today."

"I'm Ezra Dawn, and this is my daughter Scotty."

The two shake hands. "I'm Angus."

He shakes my hand next. And it's firm and warm. Calloused. "Hi."

"Is your first name Francis?" he asks. "Like the novelist's?"

Oh yes. "Yeah. But with an *e* instead of an *i*."

"Cool."

"You like Fitzgerald?"

"Uh-huh. But not as much as Hemingway."

A cute, literary bagpiper. I have died and gone to heaven. Granted, it looks like a Laundromat, but who cares?

"Are you all going to be here long? I've got to get the sheets going from the cabins."

"You live here?" I ask.

"Yeah. My parents own the campground."

"And you just happen to play the bagpipes," Dad says.

"Yeah. I was pretty excited when they decided to use our place to film a Scottish movie."

"What's your last name?" I ask.

"Matheson."

Angus Matheson.

I like it.

Dad stands up. "I've got some errands to run."

"Okay," I say.

"Maybe I'll see you around," Angus says to me. "We build a bonfire every night near the activities center. You should come over sometime. Mom does popcorn over the fire. It's nice."

"Maybe I'll come over."

Maybe? Like there's any maybe about it.

"He's really cute," I say to Dad on the way back to the TrailMama. "And has a nice voice. Kinda deep."

"Seth better watch out."

"Seth?"

"Oh come on, honey. I know you like Seth."

"Yeah, well, he's definitely proving himself to be not worthy of my time."

"True. But I feel sorry for him, don't you? He must be pretty worried about his mother."

"If he is, he's not acting like it."

And an anger rushes into me. Deep inside.

"I mean, doesn't he realize how lucky he is to have a mother at all?"

"Most people that do, don't realize that. And in a way, Scotty, mothers are supposed to be taken for granted. At least some of the time."

"I'd like to give that a shot sometime."

"You had the opportunity with Charley."

I hear some shots go off over where they're filming.

"I guess you're right."

We walk through wet grass, steering clear of anything to do with *Charlie's Lament.*

He pulls open the door of the RV. "This may not be the time to bring this up, but do you want to settle down? Maybe get a real house in Wyoming or something?"

"Wyoming?"

"Well, technically we're from there."

I shrug. "I'm not ready to say, I guess."

"We'll take all the time you need."

"Because I don't know if I can leave Charley just yet."

"I know. And that's a good thing."

Unless, of course, Charley ends up with plans of her own.

Anthony Harris?

Well, stranger things have happened.

Hollywood Nobody: May 2

Today's News: Famous director Bartholomew Evans has begun shooting his new film today near Asheville, North Carolina. He's already wreaking havoc on everybody around him. But who cares about him? The better news is that actor Anthony Harris is starring in the film. That man gets better with age! There may be romance in the air for Harris. Stay tuned!

Today's Rant: Hollywood Crime and Punishment. Is it just me, or do Hollywood stars seem to get off more lightly than us regular people? And why are there pictures of underage stars drunk and with drinks in their hands and they never get caught by the police? Isn't anyone carding them at these clubs? I don't get it.

Seth News: The Hottie is currently in North Dakota shooting his latest film with director Martin Scorsese. Seth is in the starring role. Unfortunately, according to my sources, Karissa Bonano, who's in between projects, has joined him on location. Could this be bad news for our favorite young male actor? Let's keep our fingers crossed for him.

Today's Quote: "I believe you have a responsibility to comport yourself in a manner that gives an example to others. As a young man, I prayed for success. Now I pray just to be worthy of it." Brendan Fraser

Wow. Don't you wish a lot of other Hollywood stars felt the same way?

Later!

Seven o'clock

I need to get Edie Haas's get-well card in the mail. Town is way too far for a quick trip on my scooter, but maybe I can talk Dad into running me in after the bonfire.

Yes. The bonfire.

I'm going.

I'm nervous and I've been praying and I feel a little silly for praying about something so insignificant in light of all that's going on in the world, including Mrs. Haas. But I can't help myself.

"Dad?" I call from the bathroom where I'm putting on some makeup. Not much. I don't want to freak everybody out.

"Yeah, honey?" He's reading a book about prayer. He said tomorrow morning we'll start praying together before we begin school. That'll be so cool.

"Is it okay to pray for small things?"

"Yes."

I peek my head out around the door. "Really?"

"It is. God likes to hear it all."

"How can you be so sure?"

"Because he loves us, Scotty."

"I know. But it seems so silly, doesn't it?"

"To you, maybe. But it isn't. Trust me. The last thing God wants is for you to not tell him stuff. It hinders your relationship with him. He's like me. He likes to be close."

God like my dad? That's a very cool thought.

I apply some lip gloss and step out of the bathroom. "Do I look okay?"

"You look great. Want me to walk you over?"

"Sure."

Charley bustles into the camper. "Oh, man! I'm so mad I could spit!"

Whoa, Charley.

"What happened?" Dad.

"That director. He didn't even end up using that side of beef! Said he changed his mind. Wanted roasted fowls. Anthony and I were running around all day!"

"Oh yeah?" I raise my brows.

"I know what you're thinking, Scotty, and it isn't like that. He's really really nice and all. That's all there is to it."

"Are you sure? He thought you were pretty last night . . ."

"Really?" Then she waves her hand. "Oh, never mind. Believe me, I'd be way overdoing it to think he's interested like that."

Dad takes her tote bag. "I saw it too."

"Well, it doesn't matter." She sighs. "Anyway, I've got so much to do tomorrow. And here's the thing: Evans wants the food to be edible! You know how much more time that takes."

A knock vibrates the door of the RV. I open it.

"Mr. Harris!"

"Scotty! Mind if I drop in?"

"Of course not. Come on in."

He climbs into the RV. "Hello there, Charley."

She drops her gaze. "Hi, Anthony."

"There's a bonfire going on over in the clearing near the activities center. Would you like to accompany me?"

I cross my arms. "You just want one of our chairs, don't you? Your famed chair not working out so well these days?"

He nods. "You know, I'm beginning to think I need a new lucky chair!"

"Well, my pink one is off limits."

"Shame."

"But you have your pick of the others."

"Thanks. So, Charley. What do you say?"

"Well . . . all right. I suppose."

"I'm just heading over there now," I say, grabbing a small purse I bought in Marshall, Texas, before we left.

"Splendid. Let's all go together then," he says.

"Dad? You going to go?"

He shakes his head. "I've got lots of work to do if I'm going to fly out Friday."

My stomach fills with dread. Oh man. He's really going to do it. "Okay." But I'll think about it later. I've got to get Charley and her man to the bonfire.

Fifteen minutes later

My bagpiper walks up to the blaze and stops. He arranges his pipes and begins to play and you know, it's not that bad. When he does it, standing there in a kilt, shirt, and tie, well, it all sort of goes together.

"Amazing Grace."

Even I know that song.

Amazing grace how sweet the sound
That saved a wretch like me
I once was lost, but now am found
Was blind but now I see.

Yes, I do see these days. I look around me at the world and I know God made it. I look down at my hands and I know God made them too. And I wonder what they were made to do.

"Ah," Harris sighs next to me. "That lad knows how to play a song." He reaches for Charley's hand and she lets him gather hers in his.

She needs to be loved. Oh, Jesus, just let her be loved.

I sit up straight. But what if Anthony Harris isn't as nice as he seems? I know a little about him, but not much. I'm definitely going to find out all I can about him.

Angus finishes the song. It's too beautiful to clap. We all just sit there, soaking in the silence that seems to sigh with the beauty of the melody.

Yes, another breathtaking moment here in the mountains.

But he fills the bag again, and a young woman dressed in a plaid skirt and a velvet jacket walks gracefully toward him. She favors him. Must be his sister.

He begins a rousing tune and she begins to dance. She kicks her feet with impossibly pointed toes and hops on the balls of her feet, hands sometimes on her hips, sometimes up in the air. Everybody begins to clap in time to the music.

"The Sean Triubhas," Harris says.

I'm loving this Scottish stuff.

When the song ends, she crosses two swords in a plus sign in front of her, and Angus starts again.

"The Sword Dance." Harris. "They used to do this after battles. Or so the legend goes."

And I'm thankful for his running commentary, even though I can't take my eyes off the pair. Honestly, though, I can't picture knights, or whatever, jumping around like this.

Finally it ends and a skinny woman in jeans and a sweatshirt proclaims, "Popcorn and soda in the center!"

Should I go? I mean, what was I thinking in choosing this outfit? It's so out there! A long sixties midiskirt, boots, and a suede jacket? Who was I trying to kid? I look like a wannabe soap-opera star from years gone by!

Angus files with the rest of the crowd into the center.

Do I follow the crowd? If Angus wanted me to go in, wouldn't he have come over and invited me? Maybe he was just being nice in the Laundromat. Maybe his parents tell him to be hospitable so people will keep coming back to their campground.

Maybe I should just read by the light of the bonfire before people come back with their snacks.

I pull my book out of my purse.

Harris taps my knee. "You're not going to sit here and read with all those exciting people going in for refreshments, are you? Not to mention that fine young lad."

"I don't know. I guess I'm—"

"He was eyeing you," Harris says. "Surely you saw that."

"Scotty's alone a lot," Charley says. "I think she's just nervous."

Angus emerges from the building and he's walking straight toward us.

"Looks like the laddie has taken a shine to the lassie." Harris pours on the accent.

Oh, man, did I mention how cute Angus is? Okay, he's not Hollywood. His face isn't perfectly handsome at all, but that smile he spreads when he approaches is warmer than that bonfire.

"Scotty, right?"

I nod. "Angus."

"That's me. Want some popcorn? I got my mom to put extra butter on it."

"Go ahead, baby," Charley says.

"Okay." I stand up. "I'm not one to turn my back on buttered anything."

What a stupid thing to say!

Well, it's awkward. What can I say? We don't know each other. But there's plenty to watch around us. Crew members talking about the shoot, probably about that stupid Mr. Artsy, gather in clumps of folding chairs, and in the corner sits a man playing a guitar while the dancer saws away on a fiddle. Bluegrass music is filling the space.

"My dad," Angus says.

His dad starts to sing "'Liza Jane,'" his deep voice filling the space. "He's great."

"He loves music."

"What's his name?"

"Duncan."

I laugh. "Figures."

He wears muttonchop sideburns and they're gray, like the mane of wavy hair that grows away from his face and down the back of his neck. He smiles, a warm, comforting grin that makes you want to dance a little to his song. To be honest, I think he's a bit drunk, but I'd never say that out loud.

The skinny woman in jeans approaches. "Angus. Can you play a few numbers later? I don't know how much longer your father's going to last."

"Sure, Mom."

I look over at Duncan Matheson again. A red plastic Solo cup sits beside him, and between songs he takes a healthy swig. Hmm. Wonder if there's more than soda in there.

"Who's this?" She nods at me.

"Scotty. She's with the shoot."

"Hi," I say.

"Nice to meet you."

Worry lines a mile deep divide her forehead. And her eyes are weighted down with sadness. But she pastes on a smile. "Get some popcorn while it's still warm. I'm going to go make some more. Angus, don't wander too far. We may need you."

We each fill a bowl of popcorn, grab a soda, and head back outside. Angus leads me toward a spot of grass on the other side of the fire. "Is this okay?"

"Sure."

And we eat. Just watching the flames.

Finally I can't stand it any longer. "So you like Hemingway?"

"Yeah. I know he's fallen out of favor now, but, you know." He shrugs.

"I do know." Oh, I could go on and on about *The Old Man and the Sea*, but it all feels so stupid inside my head.

"So what are you doing here with the shoot?" he asks.

Now this is something I can talk about.

He's really interested, asks intelligent questions about what it's like to be around stars and all their issues, if I ever wish for a normal life.

"Yeah, I do. A lot of the time."

"I don't blame you. I'll bet living in an RV gets old."

I want to kiss his face! I'm so tired of everybody telling me how lucky I am, how thankful I should be to have such an interesting, unusual life.

"You mean that?"

"Oh, sure. We get permanent RVers a lot here. Sometimes I meet couples who really wish they hadn't sold it all for the road. If it rolls, it's just not the same thing as home, is it?"

"No. Not even close."

"You don't even have your own room, do you?" He sips his drink.

"No. I'm in the loft over the cab."

"Class C then?"

"Yeah." This guy speaks my language! "So, do you go to school?"

"I'm homeschooled. Plus I do some online stuff with a school in Indiana. I'll be finished this year."

So no need to be embarrassed with this guy. How cool is this? "You going to college?"

"In Scotland."

"Figures!" I laugh.

"Yeah, my dad is over the top with this family-heritage stuff. But we have fun with it."

"Was that your sister dancing?"

"Yeah."

"I thought so."

We sit in the warmth of the blaze and I'm trying to think of something to say, but this is new territory.

His mother walks toward us. "Angus, I need you to take over the music. Did you bring your guitar over?"

"Sure. I'll be right there."

"ASAP. He's got to get home." She turns on her heel.

"Angus? Is everything— "

"So anyway, I was wondering if you'd like to go into town tomorrow? I can show you around."

"Well, I do have a letter to mail."

"And you shouldn't keep the person who's receiving it waiting any longer."

"It's true."

Charley steps into our view. "Ready to go back, baby?"

I nod then turn to Angus. "Thanks. This was a fun night."

"So I'll pick you up at noon and we can grab coffee too."

"Oh. Cool. Okay."

Harris walks us back home and I'm zinging. A cute guy who already seems to get me! I am so looking forward to tomorrow!

Still, I can't help but feel bad for him. It's obvious there's a lot going on at home.

3:00 a.m.

My phone vibrates under my pillow. Text message? At this time of the night?

Seth: I jst gt out of jail.
Me: What?!!!!
Seth: Undrage drnkng.
Me: What about Karissa?
Seth: She mngd 2 slp away.
Me: I'm so sorry. Are you okay?
Seth: Yea. Mad at myslf.

You should be!

Me: Are you going to tell your parents?
Seth: I clld Dad. Hes nt gng 2 tll mom.
Me: Good. She's got enough to worry about.
Seth: I cnt blve I ws so stupid.

I can! That Karissa is so evil.

Me: I don't know what to say to that.
Seth: Its ok. U dnt hve 2 sy anythng. We bth knw its tru.

Me: I'm here if you need me.

Seth: I knw. Its why I txtd u. Sctty whts hppning to me?

Me: Fame. You're not invincible, Seth.

Seth: I knw. Dnt knw wht I ws thnking.

Me: You weren't thinking. That's the problem. You need to dump the Karissa.

He doesn't text me back. And now I'm wide awake.

I might as well hop on the Internet and find out all I can about Anthony Harris. Let's hope he's not a womanizer like the John Barclay character he immortalized.

Google: Anthony Harris.

Okay. I reach behind me for my cat glasses. And to be honest, I'm getting a little tired of them. Maybe I need something new. But they're so me. It's nice having a trademark at my age.

As expected, a load of hits fills the screen, and about a hundred more screens if I want to go that long.

Okay, here's a page devoted entirely to him. It's a fan page. He doesn't have his own website. He's old school.

The bio:

> Anthony Harris was born on February 2, 1948, in Edinburgh, Scotland, along the Royal Mile in the upstairs front room of his parents' home. His father, Lowell Harris, a Presbyterian minister, ruled the home firmly but with a great deal of love. Anthony's mother, Fiona, owned a millinery shop on the first floor of the family home.
>
> He left home in 1966 for London to pursue a career in acting. The stage, however, was not to be his first love.

After appearing for four years in a supporting role in the BBC detective series, *Love and Howe*, he was hired on by director James Filmore for the role of John Barclay and proceeded to make more than ten films in the famous secret-agent series.

Other roles have come his way since then. See his entire filmography here. But Harris himself will admit his favorite roles have been Edward the Black Prince and Dr. David Livingstone. "I've always loved history. Historical films have been some of the most important. If we learn from them, that is."

Harris was married in 1970 to actress Marlena Vickers, best known for her title role in *Mrs. Cheverly*. After her death four years into their marriage, a heartbroken Harris vowed never to marry again. His secrecy about his subsequent relationships, as well as his highly guarded privacy, continues to affirm his decision in the eyes of his fans and his colleagues.

Harris currently resides in a castle near Perth, Scotland, raises milk cows, and runs an organic farm. He loves to fly-fish and collects pipes.

Vowed never to marry again? Has had subsequent relationships? How far have those relationships gone? Did he snare women only to leave them heartbroken?

What, as they say, is the deal?

There's no way I'm going to let him hurt Charley.

Thursday, May 3

Of course Charley's already gone. She has to arrange a simple supper in a small stone croft house that was built for the movie. Just bread and cheese and beer. Piece of cake after what Evans has put her through so far. And thank goodness the feast with game fowl went well. Of course, he acted like her work was subpar, but she was proud of what she did, even if she had to clean up the carcasses of "those poor birds" afterward.

Dad and I have just finished our morning prayers, and it was cool. He even bought a little book of prayers. He said a line, we said some together. I liked it.

But now I'm getting ready for my trip to town with Angus. I still can't believe it. Technically, this is my first date. If it even is a date. Is it a date? I mean, he didn't say, "Let's go out on a date," did he? Is it only official if he proclaims it a date?

I have no idea.

"Dad?"

He just printed out some sort of spreadsheet. Now he's arranging the pages in a binder. "What is it, honey?"

"I looked up Anthony Harris last night." I tell him all about it. "Should I talk to him? Ask him about his intentions?"

Dad breaks into a grin. "Oh, Scotty. Charley's an adult. She can't have you nosing around in her romantic business."

"But what if she's just another in a long string of failed relationships? And even if he does really like her, it's not like he's going to marry her or anything, is it?"

"People change their minds all the time."

I pour myself a cup of coffee and freshen his mug. "I just don't want to see her hurt."

He takes a sip. "Have a seat."

"I feel a Daddish talk coming on." But I slide into the booth anyway.

"Scotty, relationships between men and women are strange things. They can go any which way. But the thing is, at the beginning, we just don't know how it's going to end up."

"This seems pretty clear."

"Really? Maybe Harris just hasn't been swept off his feet since his wife died."

"But he could have any woman he wants!"

"Which makes it all the more difficult for him. Maybe they're just friends. You know, relationships between men and women don't have to end up as love affairs."

I have my doubts about that. "Charley doesn't deserve to be bowled over by some actor on set, and then dropped when it's all over and everybody goes home."

It's 11:50. Ten minutes until Angus arrives.

"No, she doesn't. But did you ever think she's ready to take that chance? How long has it been since she's been in a relationship?"

"Since Mom disappeared."

"Before that actually."

"Right before."

"Yes."

"I don't know what to do!"

He laughs. "It isn't up to you to do anything, honey. Let Charley dream a little, have some fun. It's not necessarily as serious as you think. And maybe she's learned a lot over the years."

"I guess." I sigh. "She did some pretty stupid things when she was young."

"True. Let's both give her the chance she needs to do something right. Maybe Harris is the one. Most likely he isn't."

"I always thought it was Jeremy, to tell the truth."

His brows rise. "Oh, dear. I forgot about Jeremy."

"He'd flip if he found out. I think he's taken Charley for granted all these years, expecting her to still be around when he finally decides he's ready."

"You really think so? I don't know. If he loved her, he'd have made a move by now."

"Not all men are like you, Dad. Not all men are ready to put the glass slipper on the girl's foot."

He grabs my hand. "I'm so glad I did."

"Me too."

So there's that. But you know, I think Jeremy would like to know somebody else is moving in on his territory.

I head outside the camper to wait for Angus, plop down in my pink chair and call Jeremy.

"Hey, kid," he says. "This is a surprise."

"We're in Asheville, North Carolina. Charley's doing a film with Bartholomew Evans."

"That guy. Can't stand him. Pretentious. I mean he's good, but he's not that good."

"I don't like him either. But guess who else is here?"

"I'm dying to know."

"Whatever, Jeremy. Anthony Harris!"

"No kidding!"

"Ever worked with him?"

"Can't say I've had the pleasure. He doesn't do much indie stuff."

"I didn't think so. He's a great guy though."

I see Angus walk out of the cabin near the activities center toward a Jeep. I don't have much time.

"He's a good actor," Jeremy says.

"I know. I was sitting next to him and Charley at the campground's bonfire last night and he was so nice."

"Oh?"

"Yeah. Funniest thing. He's been helping Charley out like crazy and then asked her if she wanted to go to the bonfire."

Angus pulls up.

"Hey, I gotta go. Talk to you later, Jeremy!"

"Okay, kid."

Mission, as they say, accomplished.

Angus jumps out of his Jeep, a very old, rusty green Jeep. The top is off.

I like it. And I'm glad my hair is in a wrap today, otherwise it would bloom to the size of a mushroom cloud.

He's wearing a navy-blue fleece, broken-in khakis, and Crocs. His wavy blond hair is lifted by the breeze, and wow, I didn't realize how blue his eyes are. They're beautiful. "Hey, Scotty. Ready?"

"I was just making a call."

He opens my door, quite the gentleman, and I'm so lovin' that. I slide inside.

He gets in.

"This your Jeep?" I ask.

"Yeah. I know it's not much, but my Dad and I got it for almost nothing and did a lot of work on the engine. It's not nice or anything but it gets me where I want to go."

"I like it. Must be nice to have that much freedom."

"It's cool. So do you want to go to Starbucks or more of a local place?"

"Oh, I'm all about the local."

"That's what I figured."

As we drive to town, he asks me what I'm reading.

"*Lady Oracle* and I hate it."

"Margaret Atwood. Never read her."

"Maybe her other books are better."

"Want to head to the bookstore after coffee?"

"Sure!"

Okay, that was a little too enthusiastic.

So now it's my turn to ask him a lot of questions.

Age: just turned eighteen.

Sports: Scottish field sports and bowling.

"Bowling?"

"It's a lot of fun and harder than you'd think."

"Oh, I never thought it was easy. I just thought it was for old guys."

"Hey, I like the old guys."

"I do too, actually."

Favorite food: steak but admits to liking cheese a lot when I tell him about my passion.

Favorite band: the Beatles.

So cool.

Favorite color: orange.

Family: one sister, Catriona, twenty, mom named Yvonne, and dad, Duncan, of course.

College accepted at: St. Andrews.

Best day ever: the day they bought the campground.

"Dad's parents died and left him some money, so they decided to leave their regular lives behind. Mom wasn't so hot on the idea, but I think she's adjusted okay. As you can see, Dad has a great time with it."

"Oh yeah." Because he's three sheets to the wind, probably.

"And he plays in a bluegrass band too. He travels too much, according to my mother."

Leaving her to run the campground. Hmm.

"He seems like such a nice guy," I say.

"That's what everybody says. A regular good-time Charlie." He's trying to take the hard edge off his voice I think, but I can hear it underneath his friendly tones. "So with him gone a lot, Mom and I pretty much run the place together."

You know, it's nice talking to a regular guy from a regular family, and I tell him that.

"Well, we're hardly what you call regular. But compared to where you're coming from, I can see how it would look like that. You must get pretty sick of the film world, Scotty."

"You've got that exactly right."

"I know it would wear on me. It seems so fake. Must be hard to find real friends."

"Do you have many friends?"

"Not really. I'm kind of a loner. I don't have time for a lot of social interaction."

"Thanks for doing this then. I'm kind of a loner too."

"Well, we loners have to stick together."

We laugh at the irony of the statement.

He pulls up to the Paris Bakery and Café. "You like pastries?"

"Oh, yeah. Especially cheese Danishes."

Man, I'm such a geek.

A few minutes later we stand before the long glass-fronted pastry cases. We choose a cheese Danish (for me), a napoleon (for him), and a strawberry tart and a chocolate croissant to share. Two espressos. And how cool is this? This is so totally a first date I would love to have. If it is a date. I mean, I don't know, right?

We spend the next two hours talking. And talking. And talking. He smiles at me as he speaks. And I smile at him. It just feels so nice to be with a guy who doesn't look at me as his little sister.

"You going to go to college when you're done?" he asks.

"I think so. But I don't know where."

"You should seriously consider St. Andrews."

"I just might."

I want to tell him about my life, my past—or should I say my crazy family's past. But I can't reveal our identity. I can't say a word.

That totally sucks.

Guess I just have to be the person I seem to be. Which is fine. I've never really pretended to be anybody else, have I?

When he drops me off he says, "I had a great time, Scotty."

"Me too."

"I don't know any girls like you."

No freaky weirdos? What a shock.

"Thanks. I hope."

"It's a compliment. Believe me."

I take a chance. "What made you ask me to go to town?" I don't want to say ask me out. That might be assuming too much.

He shrugs. "You looked so classy and beautiful standing there when I was playing my pipes on the field. And then, well, I found out you like to read. Who can resist beauty and intelligence?"

Did I say I like this guy?

"So, let me turn that back around on you. Why did you say yes?"

"You like books and you have really great hair. And the kilt doesn't hurt either."

He laughs. "So want to do our schoolwork together tomorrow? You can come to the house or the activities center. Or I could come here."

"How about if you come here? My dad's leaving town and I'll be a little sad."

"You close to your dad?" he asks.

"He's the best, Angus."

"Nice. You're lucky."

I place my hand on the door handle.

"Not on your life," he says. "I'll help you out."

I wait until he comes around to my side of the Jeep. This guy is just too good to be true.

I practically float inside the RV.

"Good time?" Dad asks.

"The best. He's so cool, Dad."

"I'm sure he is."

"And really cute."

"Naturally."

"Where's Charley?"

Dad raises his brows. "She and Anthony went to dinner together. Some vegetarian place in town."

"Dad— "

"Scotty, we talked about this."

"I know." I reach into the fridge for some limeade. "Okay,

we've got to talk about tomorrow. What time are you leaving?"

"Early flight."

I pour myself a glass, hold the pitcher toward Dad, who shakes his head. "Are you sure about this?"

"Positive."

"Just promise me you won't do anything stupid."

"That I can definitely promise."

"And you'll have to tell me about everything." I set my drink on the shelf near my bed and hop up into the loft.

"Everything."

I open my laptop and set to my schoolwork. It's gonna be a long night. It was so much easier with Charley when I was in the parenting role.

My phone rings at nine.

"Scotty, it's Edie Haas."

"Mrs. Haas! How are you? I just sent you a card!" I lay aside my sociology book.

"Oh, that's so nice of you." Her voice sounds a million miles away.

"Are you doing okay?"

"Just tired. Chemo really takes it out of a gal."

"I'm really sorry."

I'm whispering. Dad's already asleep, resting up for tomorrow's big trip.

"Thank you, sweetie."

"How long do you have to be on it?"

"About six weeks, I guess. Listen, I called to see if you'd heard from Seth recently."

Crap.

"Uh, yeah. He texted me this morning."

"Is he okay?"

"He's up to his neck on that movie, but yeah, he's . . . okay."

That sure is the truth. Nothing more than okay. Not swell. Not good. Not fabulous or stupendous or sensational. He's not even close to great.

And he could be so great! That's what kills me about this.

"Oh, good. I haven't heard from him in over a week and I was starting to get a little worried. He called his father but it was so brief, Steve said there's wasn't really much to report."

"No need to worry. He's alive and kicking."

That sure is the truth, too. Only I wish the kicking was him kicking the Karissa out of his life. Or me giving him a swift kick in the behind.

"All right. Well, it's getting late and I'm a little tired. It's nice to hear your voice, Scotty."

"Yours too, Mrs. Haas."

We ring off and I'm so mad I could scream.

I climb down from the loft, shimmy into my jeans and sweater, and decide a walk in the crisp mountain air might clear my head.

In the darkness, I think about my times with Seth on the beach at the Outer Banks this time last year. Working on his first real film, unsure, so nice, and did it ever seem like Hollywood wouldn't get to him. I was so wrong!

And what do I see in him?

Angus was great, don't get me wrong. I really, really like him. But these stupid feelings for Seth are still there.

I need to forget about him. I just do.

For one, he's too old.

For two, he's a working guy. I'd never get to see him.

For three, he's way too impressionable even if he wasn't too old and never around.

But before I forget about him, I've got one more message to send him. I pull out my phone and text him.

> Me: Tell Karissa good night and call your mom, you jerk!

I turn off the phone. He won't reply. And even if he does, I just don't want to read it right now.

The campground has a little white chapel not far from the shoot. I've had some pretty amazing things happen in churches, so I might as well go over. Jesus talks to me when I'm alone in churches. It's kinda crazy, and I wouldn't tell too many people about it. They'd think I was a lunatic.

Well, they'd be right. I am sort of loony. But that's beside the point.

Thankfully, I find one of the red double doors is open, and I slip into the darkness.

Oh, Lord! Help Mrs. Haas, I pray as I sit down on the back pew, all the way in the corner. And I don't feel silly praying *this* prayer at all. And help Charley while you're at it, if you don't mind. Don't let her do anything stupid.

I lie down on the pew, moonlight from a nearby window falling over the tip of my shoe. And here's something I'm learning about God: he usually gives us only enough light to make the next step, not enough to illumine the entire room.

A sense of thankfulness comes over me. For my dad. For Charley and Grammie and Grampie. And even Seth. He's not so bad. He's just too trusting and fame is coming way too soon. He doesn't know how to handle it. I ask God to help him with that.

Some time later

Whoa. I must have fallen asleep. How long has it been?

I whip out my cell phone and check the time. Oh good, only twenty minutes have passed. More time to just lie here in the chilly darkness. I like this. Just being peaceful and expecting nothing of myself and so much of God.

A sound touches my ears. A sob.

I sit up as quietly as I can.

Another sob. Then a few more.

There on the front pew, somebody's crying. This is a good place to cry. I don't blame him. His broad shoulders are hunched and I can only see the back of his neck, his head is hung so far down. He rises up and groans, looking at the ceiling.

It's Angus.

Oh, no. What happened? And he probably came to be alone and here I am.

I stand up and tiptoe toward the door.

"Scotty?"

I turn around. "I'm sorry. I was just laying back there praying and I fell asleep. I really don't mean to interrupt you, Angus."

"It's okay." He wipes his eyes with the sleeve covering his forearm. "I didn't know you were here."

"I know. You want me to leave?"

He shakes his head.

"What happened?" I ask.

I take a step forward and he doesn't stop me. So I continue on down the aisle.

I sit next to him. "What happened?" I ask again.

"I got some really bad news. I mean, I figured it would come someday. But not today."

"Oh no." Sitting in the dark, I wait for him to go on. If he wants to, he will. If he doesn't, that's okay too. He deserves to make that call.

Finally he says, "My parents are getting a divorce."

"Oh, Angus!"

"Yeah. They told me today."

"When?"

"After my graduation dinner. Mom made my favorite foods and we talked about St. Andrews. Afterward they called me and my sister into the living room and told us."

"Did they say why?"

"I'm getting older now. Mom's been unhappy for a long time, but she was just waiting around for me to grow up."

"Wow."

"She's never liked it here."

"You sort of said that earlier today."

"Yeah. And Dad just kept pushing things. He didn't even try to see things from her perspective."

"Is that what she said?"

"Uh-huh. And he didn't disagree."

"So she's the one divorcing him?"

He nods.

"Angus, I'm really sorry."

"But there's more to it. Dad's an alcoholic."

"I thought so."

"Yeah, it's pretty evident. They've been in counseling for a couple of months, but she's not trying."

"Neither is he, if what I thought was in the red cup is right."

"Yeah. She said she was just waiting until I was older to leave. I feel bad that they waited around for me."

"Don't. It's okay they did that."

"But shouldn't they have tried to be happy? How many years have they wasted?"

"You're not a waste. They did it for you."

"I don't know what they were thinking."

"Angus, something had to break in the situation. Something your mom couldn't take any longer."

He adjusts his position on the pew. "It's my dad's fault. I know that. Mom had an alcoholic father and Dad wouldn't stop drinking. Scotty, he's drunk every night. During the off-season, Mom goes to her room to watch TV and Dad stays in the family room drinking his bourbon."

"Is he mean when he's drunk?"

Angus nods. "Yeah. I learned to stay away from him after he beat the crap out of me when I was six."

"I'm so sorry!" God? Where have I been all my life? Why have I been so protected? I'm not complaining. I just feel so clueless!

"So what's going to happen?"

"My mom's moving away in the next couple of days. She doesn't want to be around for another summer season."

"Where's she going to go?"

"Back home to Richmond."

"She's going to just *leave* you?"

He crosses his arms across his chest and looks up at the chapel ceiling. "It would almost be easier that way. They told me I have to pick which parent to go with."

That's horrible!

"But how are you sup—"

"I don't know." He shakes his head. "It's no-win. If I stay here, I'm hurting the person I love most in the world. If I leave, I'm saying good-bye to the best life. I mean it's hard work. But I love this place. The mountains, the skies. I'm outside all the time, practically. There's my pipe band. Shoot, Scotty, besides my dad, this has been a great life."

"It's so unfair."

"I know."

"No wonder you were crying." Oh man, I shouldn't have said that.

But he doesn't mind. "Yeah. No wonder. I mean, I saw this coming years ago. They didn't live together, they existed together. But now it's actually happening and there's nothing I can do."

"Want to go for a walk?"

"Maybe that would clear my head."

We walk past the buildings into a clearing and up to the ridge that overlooks the city. I sit down on the grass. He lies down beside me. We are quiet under the close stars.

The moon shines on the tear tracks that stem from the outer corners of his eyes down into the grass.

"Oh, Angus. I'm so sorry."

I reach down and settle my fingers atop his head. His hair is soft and the curls are so fine. "I'm sorry," I whisper, pulling my hand away.

He reaches up and grabs my fingers, pulling my hand back to his head. "Don't stop."

"Okay."

My heart breaks for him. What kid deserves something like this?

Hollywood Nobody, May 4

Today's Rant: Why do we care about what Hollywood is doing? Who cares if the same screwed-up people are in rehab again? Who cares if rich spoiled people keep making mistakes while amassing large fortunes, which they use to buy tons of stuff instead of doing much to help anyone? I mean, percentage-wise. Hollywood itself could probably alleviate extreme world poverty if they all decided to live on $200K a year and give the rest away.

I'm just sayin'. I really am.

Nobodies, I don't have much to say today. I'm tired of hearing about people screwing up their lives.

Later.

7:30 a.m.

Well it's true! I am tired of it. I thought this blog was such a great idea, but maybe we love their bad behavior too much. Maybe the Hollywood blogosphere and the tabloids only encourage stars to keep trucking down the highway to self-destruction.

I set down my laptop and throw on some clothes.

Angus came by earlier and said we couldn't meet. He had to help his mom pack.

"Help your mom pack? Do you really have to help her do it?"

He shrugged. "I just have to."

"Okay."

And he left without making plans to get together again. Not that I blame him. He's got way too much on his mind.

But now I'm headed over to the set, even though I shouldn't be. I throw on tan cords, a black T-shirt, and the crushed-velvet blazer. A striped head wrap will have to do. I can't bear to think of trying to comb this mess on my head into a ponytail or a bun or something.

I look around me. Dad's gone. I just sort of groan God's way as a prayer for his protection. A part of me is frightened, a part of me is excited, a part of me can't wait to hear what happened. But mostly I'm frightened, and when I think about it my stomach feels sick.

I find Charley in her kitchen trailer baking biscuits. "They have to be nice and hard, like the kind the Scottish soldiers would eat before the battle."

"Nice."

"Did you know the Scots fought the Battle of Culloden after marching all night and only eating one of these things?"

"No wonder they lost. And where did you find out about the history of that?"

"Anthony. He was telling me all about it last night."

I cross my arms and lean against the sink. "And? How was it?"

"We had a good time."

"That's it? That's all you're going to say?"

"A nice time?"

"How about 'a great time'?"

"Okay." She grins. "Baby, he's such a neat man."

"I talked to Jeremy this morning."

She reddens. "Oh?"

"Yeah. Told him about the shoot, about Anthony Harris being here."

"Did you . . . ?"

"Did I what?"

"Oh, nothing. So how is he?"

"The same old Jeremy. Called me *kid* a thousand times and was glad to talk for about thirty seconds."

She laughs. "Isn't it nice how some people stay the same?"

"Yep. That's Jeremy for you."

I watch Bonnie Prince Charlie and his advisers spread land maps out on the field table, point to things on the parchment, and say their lines. Anthony Harris and Liam Neeson are the only convincing ones of the bunch. Whoever's playing Charlie looks more like Bonnie Prince Justin Timberlake.

Evan Bartholomew is such a twit. What was he thinking getting all onto Charley when he cast so poorly for the lead character?

But the older actors carry the younger guy, and soon they break down the set.

Anthony Harris comes right over in his kilt and broadsword. "Scotty! I'd like you to meet Liam."

Oh. My. Gosh!

"Okay."

Why didn't I put makeup on or do my hair or something?!

He introduces me to the tall, beautiful blond Irishman who says it's a pleasure to meet me. Like I'm so sure.

"Meet up at the pub in town tonight?" Liam asks Anthony.

"Perhaps later. I've got a date."

A *date*?!

At least he's not as oblique about it as Angus was.

"Cheers, then." Liam winks at me. (And I'm *starstruck*? What's up with that?) Then he walks off looking regal with that square set of his shoulders and that impossible jaw line and nose going right along with him.

"So, Scotty, can I interest you in a bottle of water at the canteen?"

"Sure." Maybe I can get the straight scoop.

I accompany him, wishing I was wearing some long dress with an apron and a little drawstring bag hanging at my side or something.

He hands me a water and we sit at the picnic table, where he draws out a pipe and a tobacco pouch from the pocket of the costume's jacket. "I certainly wish I had your pink chair."

"It's a great chair."

"So I guess you're wondering about my intentions with your grandmother."

"What?"

"Am I right?"

"Well, yes, but I know I haven't let anything on."

"True enough."

"And you've only gone out a couple of times."

"That's right."

"And you are a big star. You date lots of women."

"Well, that's overstating it a bit." He grins, then pulls some tobacco from the pouch and sprinkles it into the pipe. "Your grandmother tells me how smart you are. That you spend a lot of time researching this and that on the computer."

"She's right."

He tamps down the tobacco with his thumb, then sprinkles in some more. "So I'm assuming you've done a little research on me, then."

"You're right about that, Mr. Harris." I unscrew the top off the water bottle.

"Now I don't know what is on the Internet concerning me, but I'm assuming there's the official story of my wife dying."

"Yes." I take a sip and look at the bottle. Clear Mountain Water, it says. They probably shipped it from some mountain two thousand miles away from the one we're standing on.

"What did it say exactly?" He pulls out a box of kitchen matches.

"That she died four years into your marriage and you vowed never to marry again because you had been so in love with her."

"That's the story."

I make the quotation mark sign with the first two fingers on each hand. "'The story' or the story? There's a big difference."

He raises one hand and mimics my action. "'The story.'"

"So am I presuming too much to believe you're going to tell me the real story?"

"Let's take a walk, shall we?"

"Okay."

He strikes the match, holds it to the tobacco, and puffs the whole affair to burning.

"First of all," he says as we take to a path leading down the mountain toward the gate of the compound, "the part about my loving Fiona dearly is all true. She was a great lady."

"I saw. Quite respected."

"Aye. But she was more than her acting accolades. She was a lovely person. Loved to cook good meals and go for walks, much like we're doing now. We lived a rather quiet life when we weren't working."

"I have to admit, there isn't much about it on the Internet, not to mention the fact it was a *long* time ago."

He laughs. "It was that. I feel quite old right now."

"It's okay. It is what it is."

He laughs even harder. It's very jolly. "She was killed on set when a heavy light fell atop her head."

"Oh no!"

"She received quite a head injury, sustained massive damage, and died three days later having never come to consciousness. Do you know what her last words to me were?"

I shake my head.

He puffs his pipe. "She went out the door that morning. We were living in London and she was filming in one of the studios there, which made it convenient. I was sitting at the breakfast table reading the *Times*, in between shoots myself and getting ready to head back up to Scotland for a fishing trip. She said, 'Now make sure you catch the right fish. Part of it is knowing which ones are worth it, Harris.'"

"She called you Harris?"

"Aye, she did that."

"Well, I call you Harris too, around the RV."

"Do you see where I'm going with this?"

"You've just been waiting for the right fish?"

"I suppose that's exactly what you could say."

"But you've only known Charley for a couple of days. Are you saying she's the right fish?"

"I don't know if she is or not. She seems a worthy catch, though, Scotty."

"But you've had other catches."

"No. Not really. I've spent more time skimming my eyes over the pond. Acting is a tough business on relationships."

"Tell me about it."

"Oh, have you lost in love already at your age?"

"Nah. But I have a friend who's doing it all wrong. He's an actor."

We're almost to the end of the drive.

"Is he any good?"

I nod. "Actually, he is. He'll go far if he doesn't let the whole scene destroy him first."

"Is that what he's doing?"

I tell him about Seth not calling his mom. "I mean, it was one thing, him falling for Karissa and all the partying, but not calling your mom when she's sick goes beyond even common decency."

"I have to admit it sounds a little callous."

"A little?"

"It's hard to know what's in his heart, Scotty."

I stop dead in my tracks by the campground sign. My blue eyes look right into Anthony Harris's. "Can somebody, anybody, *please* tell me that sometimes people do bad things and there's no excuse for it? Isn't it okay to say that? I mean, would you recommend me acting like that if Charley got sick?"

"Of course not. What he's doing to his mother is terrible. But he's her son. Not yours."

"What if he just needs somebody to talk some sense into him?"

He pulls smoke out of his pipe and blows the cherry-sweet smell into the sky. "Is that your job, Scotty? Will he actually listen to you?"

I shrug, putting my foot up on the bottom railing of the fence. We both lean forward on it, looking into the woods. "Maybe not."

"Your grandmother tells me you have faith in God."

"She did?"

"Aye. Maybe you just need to let God take care of Seth."

"But— "

"God's not doing it the way you would?"

"Exactly! Why let people go through so much crap?"

He laughs. "There is a lot of that to go through in life, isn't there?"

"I mean, it's one thing when it's foisted upon you. Like your wife dying, or Angus's parents getting a divorce. But Seth's got every golden opportunity and he's throwing them all away."

"There's the rub."

"Yes, Mr. Harris. There's the rub exactly. So back to Charley.

What you're basically saying is that you don't know where it's going at this point, but your intentions are pure?"

"Aye. That's it exactly."

I put forth my hand and we shake. "I'll hold you to it. And don't think for a minute I won't. I'll be watching very closely."

"Indeed, I hope you will."

Should I warn him about Jeremy?

I look at his kind face, the laugh lines made deeper by his smile. "Are you a good man, Mr. Harris?"

"I try to be."

"Then I guess we'll just have to wait and see what develops between you and Charley. I'll try not to stand in your way."

"Thank you."

Why tell him about Jeremy? I mean, Jeremy knows something's going on, but hey, the ball, as they say, is now in his court.

11:00 a.m.

I pull up my English lesson online and begin a paper on *Lady Oracle*.

My in-box zings and I look through the latest round of e-mail. There are some nasty comments in there already from today's blog. People don't want to be told their obsessions might not be healthy. Shoot, it's my obsession, too, but that's beside the point, right? At least to them it is.

But one comment really jumps out at me.

"You sit there criticizing Hollywood for their consumption

and presumed inaction and what do YOU do to help the hungry and the sick? How about casting the log out of your own eye before examining the splinter in everyone else's?"

Wow. So tell me how you really feel, missie loo.

Although her words sound like something Jesus said.

I hop onto the Christian RVers chat room and see if my friend Maisie is there. She's not. I mean, she doesn't hang around all day online like I do. She's got a real life. I pop her a private message.

Maisie,

The plank in your eye, splinter thing Jesus talked about. Any insights?

Scotty

Hit send. And there we go.

By noon, I've gotten all of two paragraphs written for the two-page *Lady Oracle* paper, and the pangs of lunchtime are calling me away from this torture. I hop down from the loft and peer into the refrigerator. Dad left some corn chowder.

Uh, okay then.

I decide to head over to the activities center, where they serve up three squares a day. Maybe I'll run into Angus, just see how he's doing. Maybe he'll want to run into town and get a cup of coffee, or even just take a walk.

I seem to be taking a lot of walks lately.

Ten minutes later

I pay the five bucks for the meal, pick up a tray, and get in line at the cafeteria. Sloppy joes, hot dogs, chips, mac 'n' cheese (nice), salad, green beans. Serve yourself.

So I do. Loading up on the mac 'n' cheese and the salad. Blue-cheese dressing and loads of pepper.

Angus is wiping off tables, really working that rag in circles, as if he's trying to wipe away what happened to him yesterday. I head over toward him.

"Hey, Angus."

He straightens up. "Hey, Scotty."

"Just wanted to see how— "

"I'm fine. Hey, I can't talk. Kinda busy."

He walks away. Stalks away is more like it.

I was stupid to even come here, and this mac 'n' cheese looks like throw-up sitting on my plate. Sorry. It does. I take it up to the dish line, set it on the conveyer belt, and head out the door.

Angus's mom comes through and I step out of the way, saying nothing. What happens when a family falls apart? The other night Angus said, "I just pictured them as old people, both alone. I just figured they'd grow old together."

"Is there any hope they'll get back together?"

"None. Mom was actually ready to leave last year. I think they gave it a try for my sister and me. But it's over, Scotty. Our family is finished."

No wonder he's acting like he is. Who can blame him? I wouldn't want to talk to anybody either. Least of all somebody who can't begin to understand.

1:00 p.m.

The campground pool isn't filled up yet. The deep end contains a foot or two of water, brown leaves, and black gunk down at the bottom. I push up the lock on the gate and swing it open. This is a good place. Quiet, contained, yet still outdoors. The largeness of the mountains is starting to get to me, the girl who's used to the confines of an RV.

I plop my soccer-mom chair in the shallow end and pull out Elaine, my diary, although she's the last person I feel like talking to. I just felt like I had to bring something. I lay the diary, a leather journal with a ribbon placeholder, on my lap.

The sun shines warm on my face. I take off my cat glasses and set them in the cup holder sewn into the arm of the chair, lean back, and close my eyes.

That commenter on my blog was right.

What do I really know about anything? What do I really do? I mean, I help people when I can. Joy Overstreet on Ocracoke, Grace in Texas. But I make judgment calls all the time about people I don't even know. The problem with judgment calls doesn't have anything to do with whether their behavior is right or wrong. It's wrong of Seth not to call his mom; it's wrong of Angus's parents to lay that kind of decision in his lap; it's wrong of Britney to expose her private parts to the world; it's wrong of Lindsey to drink so much. There's no getting around it.

But Jesus told us not to judge or it would be turned right back around on us someday. And believe me, we all do bad things, so the spyglass of judgment is sure to come our way over something or other.

I guess what we can't do is pull ourselves away and not love people who do wrong things. At least if we're trying to follow Jesus anyway. Yesterday I read in 1 Corinthians that love never fails. Do I have one ounce of love for the people I write about on my blog?

Nope.

And that's wrong. Just like they're wrong for taking drugs and buying $700 shoes when kids are starving all over the world. Oh boy. It's never easy, is it?

It's so hard deciding what is right and what is wrong without looking down on those who haven't come to the same decision yet. Because they will. Someday Britney will realize she'll get more respect by not baring everything she owns. And Lindsay will look in the mirror and see the lines of booze weighing down the corners of her eyes and realize the reason nobody wants to work with her is not because they're jealous but because she's a difficult drunk. I mean, we all look in the mirror someday and see ourselves for who we really are. Don't we?

Because if we don't, we are the most pitiful of all.

I feel the sun soak into my head wrap and I unwind it, letting my crazy hair out for some exercise. I shake my head, lift my hair, and then lean back on my chair, letting my hair flow over the back.

I heard the words *love never fails* over and over again. My father knows what that's all about. Love didn't fail with him. He kept trying and trying to find me. Charley's love never failed either. She kept me safe, year after year.

So if love never fails, then what am I doing with Seth? Do I just send a mean text message and then disappear? The guy's mom has cancer, and yes, he's being a jerk, but that doesn't mean I can be one too.

Right?

Is it up to me to teach Seth Haas a lesson or two?

I just don't think so. Harris is right.

I used to think I knew so much. An hour ago I thought I had a lockdown on every truth. But right now, all I know is that I don't really know a thing about what either Angus or Seth is going through. Yeah, yeah, yeah. I've had my own pain, my own weird life throwing me curveballs every once in a while. But I've never seen my world falling completely apart. I don't even know what that looks like.

4:00 p.m.

On my way back from nap/introspection time at the pool, I hear some hubbub over at the set. Being the nosy person I am, I head over to see a full-blown argument between Evan Bartholomew and Jeremy Winger.

Jeremy's here?

Jeremy's here!

Are you kidding me? The man wasted no time, which could only mean one thing.

"Leave my shoot right now, Winger. You have no clearance to be here." Oh, Evans. Lighten up, will you?

Jeremy stuffs his hands in his pockets and laughs. "Clearance?

What is this, Bart? The CIA or something? The FBI? The USDA?"

USDA? Good one, Jeremy! Ha!

"I can't have you nosing around."

"Nosing around? Is that what you think I'm doing?"

Mr. Artsy puffs out his chest. "Well, I am more well thought of than you are."

Now I'm only a few feet away and I can't help myself. I let out a snickery puff of a "Yeah, *right.*"

Evans turns on me. "What are you doing here?"

"I heard Jeremy's voice." I grip the shoulder strap of my backpack.

"You know her?" he says to Jeremy.

"She's like a daughter to me."

So cool. Although I have to say, if I really was his daughter, he'd be a pretty absentee dad. I love Jeremy, but I'm just sayin'.

"Did she ask you to come here?"

"No. I just came to see her and her grandmother."

"The food stylist!"

Jeremy nods.

"She's been nothing but a ginormous pain to me."

Did he really just say *ginormous*?

Jeremy lightly grabs Evans's arm. "Come on, man. Just wanted to see some old friends."

Evans pulls away. "Keep your hands off me. And get off my shoot or I'll call the police."

I step forward. Evans glares. "Come on, Jeremy. You can come back to our RV. We rented the lot ourselves. It's out of Evans's jurisdiction."

"Good one, kid!"

Evans turns bright red, and I stick my tongue out at him as we turn and walk away.

Oh brother! Did I really just do that?

Jeremy asks if I want to head into town until Charley gets off work.

"Sure," I say as I climb into his ratty old pickup truck. "But don't expect her to be hanging around too long. She's got a date with Anthony Harris tonight."

He hops into the driver's seat. "So tell me about that, kid."

"Why do you want to know?"

"Your grandmother's my oldest, dearest friend."

"Is that all?"

He starts up the engine, a great big rumbling engine that's probably wreaking havoc on the environment, not that Jeremy would care. And shoot, our RV ain't exactly green either.

"I don't know, kid. Charley and I go so far back, it's hard to imagine us moving forward in any new sort of way."

"I never took you for someone with a lack of imagination, Jeremy."

There. That should get him.

And it does. His mouth sets in a ticked-off sort of line.

I like it.

But here's the thing: As I look out over the gentle mountains that really do look like pictures I've seen of Scotland, I think about Anthony Harris, who's only ever been kind to Charley. I doubt he'd take her for granted like Jeremy's been doing all these years. And yet Jeremy's been good to Charley, giving her jobs and contacts for more work when we were on the run, protecting us, looking out for us.

Oh, man! What have I gotten us into? Why did I call him?

Because he deserves to know what's going on. He's always been there for us, and if he wants a crack at Charley's heart, he should have one. That's just the truth.

So there.

Anthony Harris better put on his best fighting gloves is all I can say. And so should Jeremy. Because those two are going to give each other a serious run for their money!

And it's win-win for Charley.

What happens after this? Will she settle for either one? Will that leave Dad and me in Wyoming together?

Hmm. Interesting doings is all I can say.

9:15 p.m.

Charley's out on her date, Jeremy's settled into a hotel in town, and I didn't say a word about the pub meeting with Liam and Harris. Liam? Did I really just call the man by his first name? But I know Jeremy. He'll figure it out. He's got a nose for those sorts of things.

I've just been surfing 'round the Hollywood blogosphere, reading the same train wreck on each blog. Some nobody just like me giving his take on what Britney did today—probably something crazy as usual—and we act like we're shocked. Is anybody really shocked anymore? Aren't we just delighted that somebody who is rich and famous isn't perfect and is just as stupid as we are? Is that it? Or do we feel superior? I swear some of those people that come on *Dr. Phil* have had lobotomies!

I sigh.

I don't know.

I mean, there's the real problem. It's not only that I don't love these people, it's that I rejoice in their sins and their mistakes and their pain. Back to 1 Corinthians 13 again. Love doesn't rejoice in those things. It rejoices in the truth. And Jesus said he is the Truth.

Now, it's easy to rejoice in Jesus. He is love itself. I mean, where's the downside?

I need to stop hanging around online all the time, getting distracted by this silliness, watching people put themselves through tragedy after tragedy.

Maybe I need to read more. Do some kind of craft or learn an instrument or something. I'm online way too much.

An instrument. I think about that. Something I could learn to play on my own. Guitar maybe? So typical. But still cool.

Nah. Too big.

I check my e-mail. There's an answer from Maisie.

Scotty,

Great question. Jesus meant that when we judge others harshly, we open up the door for them to do that to us. I think when we look at his life, though, particularly the story of the adulterous woman (John 8), it's easy to see what he means. The Pharisees (remember them?) brought this woman before Jesus and were threatening to stone her. He said whoever had no sin could go ahead and throw the first stone.

Well, nobody's without sin. Needless to say, the woman didn't get stoned that day. But Jesus also didn't turn to her and say, "You're fine. I'm not going to tell you what to do." What he did say was that she should go and sin no more. And he loved her, Scotty. He didn't whitewash her actions, but he forgave her and gave her hope that maybe she didn't have to repeat her mistakes.

That help?

Love, Maisie

I hit reply.

Maisie,

Thanks. Yeah, that's good. I'll read John 8 for myself and get the scoop.

Hey, I want to play an instrument. Learn something on my own. Something pretty straightforward. Any suggestions?

Love, Scotty

Send.

Several minutes later

Celtic harp. Hands down. You'll love it! How are you, anyway?

Oh, so she's online now. Cool. I log onto IM and buzz her. She accepts my invitation.

LoveChild: I'm good. We're in Asheville. Where are you?

FiddleGirl: I'm in Colorado playing in a fiddle contest.

LoveChild: I'm doing okay, I guess. Just trying to figure out what I'm really supposed to be doing with my life.

FiddleGirl: What do you mean?

LoveChild: Well, I've just been thinking I've always got a lot of opinions and things to say, but what should I really do with my life?

FiddleGirl: You're in a unique situation, Scotty. It's not like you can settle down anywhere and make a difference.

LoveChild: But as followers of Jesus, aren't we supposed to want to make a difference?

FiddleGirl: Yes.

LoveChild: Okay. Well, pray for me. I think I'm wasting a lot of my time. I'm almost seventeen. I need to be thinking about the rest of my life.

FiddleGirl: Will do. Have a good night, sweetie.

LoveChild: I will. You too.

Celtic harp. Celtic harp. I hop onto an online auction site, see that the twenty-two string with levers seems to be a good starter harp, pay through PayPal, I should get express shipping because with the way Evans is acting, who knows how long we'll be here. But it's just too expensive. I'll take my chances.

It should arrive in ten days.

Saturday, May 5

No shooting this weekend. We're on union time now, baby. Jeremy could get away with a lot being Mr. Indie, but not Bartholomew Evans. He plays it safe and by the book.

Must be why he's so darn grouchy all the time!

So here's the deal. I'm taking weekends off from the online world. I'm only allowing myself to check e-mail once a day. And no blogging. Hey, the Nobodies should be out having fun, going to the park, the movies, hanging with friends, whatever. I'm the last person they need to be with. So true.

I stayed in the RV almost all day yesterday catching up on schoolwork. The fact that I didn't want to run into Angus fueled my hermit ways, I hate to say. He's in so much pain and I don't know what to do, and furthermore, I don't think he wants any contact with me. I guess I can't blame him. Okay, I'm making it about me and I shouldn't. I doubt he wants any contact with life in general right now.

I think it's late. I couldn't fall asleep last night, I was so worried about Dad. The last time I checked my cell phone it was two o'clock. It's full daylight now, I can tell, and I really don't want to get out of bed. Charley's bedroom door is shut so I think she's still asleep. She was out really late. Partying it up at an Irish pub with Liam and Harris?

Man, things can change in a flash!

I throw back the covers, my curiosity about Charley's big date last night getting the better of me. Reach for my cell phone. Ten o'clock. She is so getting up now. But I have to make it nice for her because I'm totally committed to getting lots of info out of her. There's no way I'm letting her off the hook!

So. Tea. Two cups of Assam tea with heated soymilk and raw honey. That, I'm telling you right now, will put anybody in a good mood. Sometimes Charley's healthy stuff, when assembled in the right combination, leads to something amazing.

I set the kettle on one burner and a pot of soymilk on the other. Spooning the loose tea into a diffuser, I start worrying about Dad again. What's he doing right now? Probably just walking the streets of Little Italy. The problem is, as unrecognizable as he is these days with the shaved head, the tattoos and all, he's hardly rendered himself inconspicuous.

I pull down our old teapot. Charley said it was her mother's long ago. It's the only heirloom we have. Precious stuff, made in Belleek, Ireland.

Waiting for the water to boil, I long to hop on the Internet and Google Little Italy, Baltimore, Maryland again. But I know what I'll see. Sidewalk, asphalt, and about a million restaurants with names like Amicci's (Dad's personal favorite), Vellegia's, Caesar's Den, Sabatino's, Ciao Bella, and more. But I can't Google anything. I'm on break.

This is going to be harder than I thought! My laptop just calls to me there on the dinette. And it's a nice laptop. I saved for almost a year for that thing. It roars and I like the illumined apple on the back of the silver screen too. Hey, aesthetics mean something to a girl like me.

No. I will not do it.

The water begins to boil and I do not want to wake Charley with the screaming kettle whistle, so I ready a dishrag and just before it sirens, I place the dishrag over the handle and lift it off the burner.

So what's Dad doing this morning? I pour the scalding water

over the leaves in the diffuser resting inside the neck of the teapot. Yes. That lovely old smell. Makes me feel connected to long ago.

Is Dad getting coffee at an Italian bakery? I wonder where he spent the night.

So the tea has to steep a little and that being the case, I might as well text him.

Me: Good morning, Dad. Where are you? Have you eaten breakfast?

He answers right away. Thank goodness they haven't gotten to him yet, and you know? Why did I have to love those stupid *Godfather* movies? They're really coming back to haunt me.

Dad: Yep. Had an egg mcmuffin and a cup of horrible coffee. I'm heading to LI today.

Me: BE CAREFUL!!

Dad: This is more fact-finding, honey. Nothing to worry about yet. I'll be home by tomorrow afternoon.

Me: Keep in touch regularly or I may keel over from worry.

Dad: You got it.

Me: Love you!!

Dad: Love you too. Have a good day, and don't you get in trouble either! Ha!

Me: Okay. See ya!

Dad: Over and out.

There. Okay. At least I got in "those three little words" (well, technically two, because I didn't use "I" before "love you," but that's beside the point) before somebody decides he should be "swimming with the fishes" and oh, dear Jesus! Don't let anything horrible happen to him! We just found each other. That would just be so wrong!

I pour the tea into two mugs, drop in a large tablespoon of honey into each so it all melts, and then stir in the warmed soymilk.

Okay, Charley. Prepare to meet your interrogator!

I don't believe it! She's not there.

No way. She so didn't *not* come home last night! I mean, I know Charley has a past and all, but surely one blue-eyed glance from Harris didn't make her forget all the principles she learned since I came into her life? That's just not an option.

Her big binder sits on the sofa, and I flip it open to the contacts page. There's Bartholomew Evans's cell phone number. My eyes hesitate on the name and number written in Charley's careful, yet artistic handwriting.

Hmm.

I sip my tea.

Should I?

Mr. Artsy would definitely know where Harris is staying. Or maybe she's with Jeremy? Maybe he saw her with the handsome Scot, realized he was making a big mistake keeping her at arm's length, and just swept her off her feet like she's been wishing he would do for years.

I mean yearzzzz.

Reaching up in the loft for my cell phone, first I call Jeremy. No answer. Figures. He rarely answers. He's a call-you-back sort of guy.

I consider the situation before me. For one, there could be a reasonable explanation for her absence, like she was here asleep and left early to do some shopping for next week's shoot. I might have just missed her completely. I call her cell phone. No answer.

For two, they had an accident or something and stayed in town, Harris being the consummate gentleman and booking her a room of her own at his hotel. No answer on her phone. Again.

For three, she stayed the night with Harris and I *so* don't want to even think about that!

I flip open my phone, looking back and forth several times from the keypad to Evan's number. Should I?

But what if something really bad happened to Charley?

Because . . .

For four, Harris might have been a total jerk, fooled us all with his Old World Scottish friendliness thing, and done something really bad.

And finally, for five, Charley might have decided she couldn't take our weird life any longer and just ran away. Maybe Jeremy dropped her off at the airport or something. I have no idea.

I underline Evans's number with my left index finger and dial the phone with my right thumb. Okay, Scotty, breathe deep.

You can do this.

"Yes?"

"Mr. Evans?"

"Who is this? How did you get my cell number?"

Great. Just as I figured.

"This is Scotty Dawn."

"Who? I've never heard of you."

"The food stylist's granddaughter."

He starts yelling at me and his choice of words is so cliché it's unworthy of repetition in any way, shape, or form. I'll bet this movie is going to be cliché too. He blah-blahs on about invasion of (bad adjective here) privacy and who do I think I am?

Who do I think I am?

Oh, please! The guy is a train wreck.

"I'm needing Anthony Harris's phone number."

He starts laughing. "Oh, you need my star's phone number? How quaint to even think asking something like that is information somebody like you will ever get."

"Or at least the name of the hotel where he's staying."

"Oh, that's *much* better."

"Look, my grandmother didn't come home last night. Or at least I don't think she did. Long story. I just need to see if she's all right. She had a date with Harris."

Oh no! What did I just do? I'm sure there are rules about cast and crew mixing romantically, aren't there? I mean, I don't know for sure. I'm so lame when it comes to what the big boys' rules are! I mean, Jeremy had no rules like this!

"Oh she did, did she? That's very interesting."

Crap. And does the man begin every sentence with "Oh"? I'm just sayin'.

"Can you help me?"

"Oh, you'd like that, wouldn't you?"

Good grief! The man speaks in bad movie dialogue!

"Never mind. I'll just start calling hotels asking for him, thanks."

And I quick hang up the phone. No use hanging around for another stilted line from a TV movie. What a boob!

Well, I might as well be comfortable. I grab my tea and my laptop (there's no helping it, I've got to get the phone listings) and open the door to sit outside.

Oh. My. Goodness.

There they are. Harris, leaning back in the soccer chair with his legs on the bench of the picnic table, puffing away on his pipe while Charley sits in her chair knitting. Knitting!

Knitting?

I've never seen her knit before.

"Hey, baby!" Charley chimes her cheerful morning voice at me and I want to scream.

"How long have you been sitting here?"

Harris sits up straight. As usual, he's beautifully dressed, hair combed back like a lion. "Since about eight thirty. I bought some tea and scones this morning in town and came up to share them with your grandmother for breakfast."

"Oh no." I set my tea and my computer on the picnic table. "Oh, no, no, no." I rest my head in my hand, shaking it back and forth as if a blinding headache has suddenly taken hold. Headache? I wish!

Harris stands to his feet. "Here, take the pink chair. You seem to be needing it worse than I."

"Thanks." I sit down.

"What's wrong, baby?" Charley lays down her knitting, leans forward, and grabs hold of my knee.

And at that moment, Mr. Artsy comes screeching toward our campsite, arms flying up in the air, hair like Einstein, redder in the face than Madonna must have been when she watched the first screening of *Desperately Seeking Susan*.

I am in so much trouble. Oh, man, I just want to crawl in a hole and die.

"Spill it, quickly, before he gets here." Harris.

"I called his cell phone using Charley's contacts list and asked what hotel you were staying at because I thought Charley didn't come home last night."

"Baby, you didn't!"

"Oh, I did! I did!"

Evans strides up to the camp, pointing at me. "You! You! You little idiot!"

Wow, like that so stung coming from you.

Okay, actually, it makes my heart beat even faster. I grab Charley's hand, still sitting on my leg.

Harris stays seated at the picnic table, acting like nothing unusual is going on. "Evans. What brings you out on a fine Saturday morning in the crisp mountain air?"

The point remains focused on me. "That girl. The food stylist's granddaughter." The point moves to the right, zeroing in on Charley. "She had the gall to call me on my cell phone. This little nobody."

Well, he's right, I *am* a nobody.

"She was worried. She didn't think her grandmother had come home last night." Harris reaches into his blazer pocket and pulls out his box of kitchen matches.

"So she said."

He turns on Charley. "Were you with him?"

"Well, yes, but I—"

"Then you're fired! I knew I shouldn't have hired a nobody I'd never heard of before."

There's that "nobody" again. He needs a writer beside him at all times.

"But I wasn't out—"

"With him?" He jerks his head toward Harris. "You just

admitted to it."

"No, I mean—" Charley's bright red, her ruddy face contrasting sharply with her silver-blonde hair.

Harris lights his pipe. "If she goes, then so do I."

"Mr. Harris!" I gasp.

"Anthony, no!" Charley gasps too.

He puffs nonchalantly. "Aye, it's only right, because it seems I am the root of the problem. Just couldn't keep my eyes off of you, dearie."

Dearie. How cute is that?

And what happened with Jeremy? I mean, really? Where's he today?

"You can't do that, Harris! You're under contract."

He puffs his pipe again, the blue smoke curling in the air. "We'll see about that. I'll call my attorney. Heaven knows I pay him enough, he'd better work for me on a Saturday."

"It's okay, Anthony," Charley says. "I don't want to put you in any sort of jeopardy."

"Oh, no mind there. There are always loopholes."

"Not in my contracts! Harris, you'll never eat lunch in this town again if you do this."

I can't help it. I blurt out a laugh.

Harris does too.

Charley stays grim.

"And you!" Evans turns to Charley. "You're through!"

He turns on his heel and walks away.

We watch him diminish until he disappears behind the activities center. A minute later his rental car peels out of the parking lot.

"Whew," I breathe.

"I know, baby. I can't believe it." She turns to Harris. "Are you really going to call your lawyer?"

He shakes his head. "No. It's ironclad. I can't just walk away like that. I've never done that sort of thing before and I don't actually plan on doing it now. We'll just let him sweat a bit, aye? I have a feeling by Sunday afternoon you'll have your job back."

"But he'll be so ornery!" she says.

"He can't be any worse than he's been already," Harris says. "In fact, you may find he might just mind his manners a wee bit more for all of it."

I sure hope he's right.

"Now you, young lady. You've got a bit of explaining, don't you think?" he asks.

I look straight up at the sky. "I was so worried! I didn't hear Charley come in last night and I thought the worst. Several forms of worst if you want to know the truth."

"Oh, baby."

"I was just so scared! I mean, what if something happened to you? I don't know what I'd do!"

And it's true. I love my grandmother. She raised me. I couldn't bear it if—

"Oh, baby! I'm so sorry."

I shake my head. "You didn't do anything. I mean, you came home, and you left the RV early." I look at Harris. "I didn't trust you either. I'm sorry."

Harris sets his pipe hand on the table. "I understand. Your grandmother's fortunate that you love her so much."

Charley blows out a breath full of relief. And she looks at Harris with eyes that glow like the flame of a candle.

I think she's falling in love with him.

I really do.

Sunday, May 6, 11:00 a.m.

Charley climbs up into the RV. I'm sitting on my bed reading *On the Road*, by Jack Kerouac. I figured with my lifestyle I oughta. It's one of Dad's favorites. He's read, oh, say ten novels since graduating from college, so I guess I need to remember that.

She taps my computer absentmindedly as she sits at the dinette.

"I'm sorry about yesterday," I say.

"It's okay. I didn't like working here much anyway. I miss Miss Burrell and Geo and I never realized how great it was working for Jeremy. He's so easy to work for."

"Yeah."

"And he came by the pub Friday night. He found us, I'm assuming, due to your inside information."

I shake my head. "I didn't say a word about the pub."

"Scotty."

I know, I know. I didn't have to say anything about the pub to set Jeremy on the right course. "Well, he laid low yesterday didn't he?"

"You know, baby, you're meddling a little too much here."

"I'm sorry. I know. I just can't help myself."

"You're just scared."

I'm so sick of being scared about things. "With Dad going up to Baltimore . . ."

"Uh-huh. Do you think that was such a good idea?"

I shrug. "No. But what else are we going to do? Don't you want to find Babette?"

She nods. "I do. And yet, there's the risk we could lose him, you know? And then there you'd be without your dad again. I don't know if the risk is worth it."

"But if she's alive and he makes it through okay, we'll be glad he did it."

"Yeah." She sighs. "I suppose you're right. But that's a big *if*, don't you think?"

"I do. I guess all we can do is hope for the best."

And pray. But I don't say that because I don't want to freak her out. Charley still doesn't have a whole lot of time for faith.

"Harris isn't around this morning?"

"He went to church."

"Really?"

"They have a little service in the chapel."

"Do you know when it starts?"

"Right about now, I think."

"Cool." I jump down from the loft, slide into my sneakers and hurry on over.

Harris moves over when I hurry up to his pew.

He just smiles, moves the hymnbook between us, and I get to hear his pleasing baritone voice sing the words to a hymn I've never heard before. By Charles Wesley, John's brother.

Jesus, lover of my soul, let me to Thy bosom fly,
While the nearer waters roll, while the tempest still is high.
Hide me, O my Savior, hide, till the storm of life is past;
Safe into the haven guide; O receive my soul at last.

Other refuge have I none, hangs my helpless soul on Thee;
Leave, ah! leave me not alone, still support and comfort me.
All my trust on Thee is stayed, all my help from Thee I bring;
Cover my defenseless head with the shadow of Thy wing.

I sing it as best as I can, singing it for Dad, asking God in the poet's words for all that is contained within the lyrics.

Harris and I sit quietly while the minister preaches a sermon so different from the one I heard at the tent meeting a year ago. He talks about the love of God, the all-encompassing love of God, which never ends, never fails, never ceases to intervene on behalf of his children.

I like it.

I really, really do.

At the end of the service, Angus puts on his bagpipes and plays "Amazing Grace" again, and I cry. I can't help myself. Harris sniffs beside me and it's good to know he isn't acting, that his tears are for real. Just like mine.

2:30 p.m.

My cell phone rings as I sit in my spot at the bottom of the swimming pool.

"Hello?"

"Scotty, it's Steve Haas."

"Mr. Haas! How are you? How's Mrs. Haas?"

"Ah, not too well. She started running a bad fever, so they've put her in the hospital. I'm trying my best to get hold of Seth and he's not answering his phone."

"Have you texted him?"

"What's that?"

"Never mind. E-mailed him, then?"

"Yes, repeatedly. Has he been in contact with you recently?"

"Not since I talked to your wife last week. I sent him a text message by cell phone after our conversation and told him to call home, but he never texted back."

I can hear Mr. Haas blow out a sigh. "I hope he's all right. I'm worried."

"Oh, listen. I'm sure he has to list some type of emergency contact or something on the job. If anything bad has happened, the production company would give you a call."

Right? It sounds so lame. But he grasps it. "Okay. Would you mind letting me know if he calls? Just so we know he's okay. Edie's sick with worry."

"And she doesn't need that right now. Are you at the hospital?"

"Yes, I am."

"Can I talk to her for a sec?"

"She's asleep."

"Oh. I'm sure that's for the best."

"The best is what we're hoping for."

"Mr. Haas, I'm praying for you all."

"Thanks, Scotty. Seth told me about your finding God."

"He did?"

"Yeah. He thought it was pretty cool but said he had a little bit more living to do before he settled into anything that entailed church and what have you."

Wow. Was he ever speaking the truth. Livin' it up with the

Karissa is more like it.

We ring off, and all my good intentions regarding Seth have been flushed down the toilet. I can't believe he *still* hasn't called his mom.

One hour later

I scream with joy as Dad pulls up to the RV. He gets out and I jump up into his arms. "Dad!"

"Scotty!"

Man, he feels so good. My dad.

Charley's head appears in the doorway of the RV. "Oh, Ezra, you're back. What a relief!"

Dad sets me down, reaches into the cab of the truck for his backpack, and I escort him into the RV, zinging with happiness. He's safe. He's back here. Thank you, God!

Charley stirs a pot of soup she just made for dinner. Vegan cream of broccoli, "cream" being the euphemism here. "Can I make you some coffee, George?" (The door's closed now, so we can call Dad by his real name.)

"No offense, Charley. But I'll go ahead and make it myself. It usually takes a coffee drinker to make good coffee." The fact that Charley's just recently taken up drinking the stuff disqualifies her, apparently.

"Not a problem."

He busies himself with the grinding of beans and I slide into the dinette. "So. Tell me everything. What happened? Did you meet anybody helpful? Find out any information? I want to hear every last detail."

He laughs. "As if that's a shock." He presses down on the grinder and that high-pitched squeal erupts as coffee beans lay down their lives for joyful human consumption.

Finally. "Okay, so I was hanging around an Italian bakery and coffee shop Saturday morning."

"Which one?"

"Not saying. Trust me on this, honey. The less you know the better."

"Darn."

"Really. To make a long story short— "

"Dad!"

"To make a long story short, I was reading the *Sunpaper*, which, of course, had an article about Robertsman's campaign, him being a local boy and all. I was sitting near a table full of old men sipping on espresso. So I rapped the paper, put on a New Jersey accent and said, 'I'm from outta town. This guy a real front-runner around here? Never heard of 'im.'

"Well, they started in. And of course some hated the guy and others loved him. I said, 'With a name like Robertsman? Not hardly from the old country.' And they laughed."

He slides the pot into the coffee maker, presses the button, and the gurgle begins. "So anyway, to make a long story short— "

"Dad!"

"To make a long story short, one of the guys stayed behind and sat at my table and I asked, with a joking kind of tone, if he or Robertsman could recommend a good restaurant around here for dinner."

"What did he say?"

"He gave me his favorite restaurant, winked, and said Robertsman's been eating at Mama Agnese's for years."

"Still!"

"Right."

"So you went over there for dinner last night?"

"Well, sort of. I went to the maître d' and asked if they were hiring."

"No way!"

"Oh, George, no!" Charley says. Her hand, reaching for a yellow squash, stops midair.

"I did. Told them a story about needing work on Friday and Saturday nights. Wife gone and trying to raise my daughter on my own."

I shake my head. "Well, at least you made it as truthful as you could."

"What? I really do need that job to find out what I can!"

"True."

"So anyway, there you have it. I'm going to have to fly out earlier on Fridays than I thought. But I'll just have to burn the midnight oil during the week to get my real job done."

He looks so real and nice sitting there. I sit next to him, lay my head on his shoulder, and breathe him in. Ten minutes later, the coffee maker, finishing up, lets out what we call the "three significant beeps," signaling it's time to drink up.

As Charley finishes up dinner, I sit outside with Dad.

"Want me to build a campfire tonight?" he says.

"Sure." I can't seem to take my eyes off my feet.

"What's the matter, honey?"

"What if something bad happens to you? I mean, this could get dangerous, Dad. Really dangerous. And then I might lose you too."

He rises from his chair and leans down on his haunches in front of me. "If your mom's alive, she deserves to know that we're still alive too. She deserves the chance."

"I know. But I'm scared." I whisper, feeling tears prick the backs of my eyes. I will them away.

"Scotty." He lays gentle hands on my forearms and squeezes. "We have to find out what's happened to her. I promised so many things to your mother when I married her." He clears his throat. "She's the love of my life. If she needs to be rescued, even if it's just from the lies she was told about our demise, then I have to do it. Can you understand that?"

"Yeah. But it still frightens me."

"Trust God, honey. It's all we can do."

"But sometimes God lets bad things happen to people, Dad. It's true!"

"Yes, it is. But that doesn't keep us from doing the right thing. Or it shouldn't."

"I know. It's just hard."

"You're right."

Charley leans out the door. "Supper!"

Ten minutes later

When we're halfway through our meal, the trailer door vibrates under a brisk knock. It opens and Jeremy stands there.

"Hey, Jeremy, come on in," I say, trying to act all nonchalant. "Want some supper?"

"Sure, Jeremy! Come on in." Charley.

Dad gets up and pulls the only real chair we have in the RV over to the table. "Have a seat."

Dad and Jeremy got along fine when they met at the last shoot.

"Thanks."

"So how are you doing today?" Charley asks.

"*What* have you been doing today?" I ask.

Dad spoons out a bowl of beans and a plate of squash and sets them down at the end of the dinette.

Jeremy sits down. "Just scoutin' around the place, kid. This could be a good spot for the next shoot on my lifetime project."

"Oh, that!" Charley rolls her eyes.

Whoa. That's so not her!

See, Jeremy's been filming bits and pieces of something that will, supposedly, all make sense years from now when he pieces it all together. Our last shoot was the latest leg of that journey, a horror piece in which the Karissa screamed herself silly. She's good at the silly. And good at the screaming, most likely because she hears people around her doing it so much at her antics.

Jeremy shrugs and digs into the beans. "These are good. As usual. But then you've been making great food for years."

Oooh. Nice. Appeal to sentimentality. I like it.

"So what are you doing around these parts?" asks Dad.

"Just scouting. Scotty told me you all were here, so I figured why not?"

More small talk occurs as we finish up the meal. Finally, as Dad and I clear the plates to do the dishes, Jeremy clears his throat. "Uh, Charley, can I talk to you privately? You wanna take a drive or something?"

"I have to be back by seven. Anthony is picking me up then."

"Will do."

A minute later, the throaty rumble of his old truck leaves us behind.

"Wow, Dad."

"I know. What do you think he's going to say?"

"With Jeremy, it's anybody's guess."

9:00 p.m.

After our campfire, I can tell Dad's beat, and I don't blame him for wanting to go to bed. I'm tired too. Worry really tires a person out! Seth, Mrs. Haas, Angus and his family, Charley and her paramours. My goodness! So much drama right now.

I figure I'd better try Seth again, so I text him.

> Me: I came off a little harshly. Your dad called today and both he and your mom are sick with worry. Your mom is in the hospital. High fever. Please, please, please call home. Is this phone even working? I hope for your sake it isn't.

I wait until nine thirty and figure an answer isn't forthcoming. So okay then. I'd better get some science done or I'll never finish out the year by June.

When I finally turn out my light an hour later, the RV is only illuminated by the hood light over the range. It's peaceful.

My window is opened slightly and I hear the sounds of the night woods behind me. And I pray for everybody I can think of in the world that I know and some that I don't.

After a while, that blog comment comes back to me. "What do *you* ever do for anybody?"

So I add one last prayer. "Okay, God," I whisper. "Show me what you want from me. What it really means to act like a Christian, not just feel like one or think that I am one. What is it we're supposed to be doing around this planet you chose to leave us on?"

As I'm drifting off to sleep, still feeling peaceful and thinking that surely that is a prayer God will answer, Charley softly enters.

"Charley?" I whisper.

"Go back to sleep, baby. I'll tell you what happened in the morning."

"Will we be pulling out soon?"

"No. Evans called me earlier and offered me my job back."

"Then wake me up before you go."

"Okay. I love you, baby."

"Love you too."

She clicks off the hood light.

It's good to be loved. It really is. Even if she won't tell me what happened with Jeremy. Or Harris.

It's weird having the popular girl for your grandmother.

I can't help it. The thought makes me smile. Right here in the dark.

Monday, May 7

Despite the fact that Charley left without telling me what Jeremy said, it's a good day. I would say it's good to be back on the Internet this morning, but it's not. I'm getting tired of the whole blog world.

Dad, across from me at the dinette, takes a sip of his coffee. "Getting lots done?"

"Nope."

"Can't concentrate?"

"I wish!"

He doesn't know about the blog.

"Why don't you go take a walk? Clear your head a little bit?"

"Okay."

Like he has to talk me into that.

So I change out of my pajamas into a pair of wool trousers from the forties, a black twinset from the fifties, and I scrape my hair back into a bun like I've been doing lately. I set my cat glasses on my nose.

"I'm heading out, Dad."

"You look nice. Planning to run into that bagpiper?"

"I don't know. He's going through a rough time. I think he needs to be alone these days. His parents are splitting up."

"What a shame."

"I know. All right, I'll be back in a few."

I head over to the activities center because maybe, just maybe he'll be around.

Sure enough, I spy him carrying a box from his home to a U-Haul truck. Oh, man.

Jesus, do I go on over? Am I really the last person he needs to see right now?

Go.

I feel the answer in my heart.

Okay, then.

I approach. "Angus!"

He turns as he steps out of the truck. "Hey, Scotty."

"Want some help?"

"You don't look like you've got the right clothes on."

"It's about the shoes." I hold up my foot and its black clog.

"Okay. Suit yourself."

Well, with a reception like that, how can I not?

I follow him into the house. The living room contains only a couch and a coffee table.

"She's taking the chairs. They were nice chairs. Wingbacks." He shrugs. "I read *The Sun Also Rises* and *The Great Gatsby* in those chairs."

Moving boxes are lined up along the wall, through which a doorway exposes kitchen cabinets in the other room.

I heft one and head out the door. "Where are your mom and dad?"

"At the lawyer's office signing some paperwork."

I nod—less said the better—and deposit the box on the lip of the truck's trailer. "I'd better let you do the arranging."

"Thanks." He steps up into the truck. "I can't believe it."

"I'm sure. Is she leaving today?"

He nods. "As soon as the truck is packed."

"We can take our time." I half smile.

He half smiles back. "Wish that would work. Man, this just makes it all so real. I thought it was real yesterday and the day before. I even thought it was real months ago when I realized it would happen eventually. But none of that felt real compared to this."

We cart more boxes from the house, and about thirty minutes later the task is finished.

"She can get her own clothes," he says.

"Yeah."

"Do you want a soda or something?"

"I am a little thirsty."

He heads back to the kitchen and returns with two cans of root beer. "This okay?"

"Sure." I pop the tab. "Wanna go somewhere else?"

"Anywhere but here."

We walk past the activities center, skirt the shoot with a wide berth, and head onto the path up to the top of the mountain. We find the clearing we sat in a few nights ago, but today the sun shines and a thin veil of wispy clouds pass by in the wind. We sit down.

"I hate him," he says, his face set like a stone.

Whoa.

"And I hate her too."

I just sit there, not saying anything. Dad told me, when talking about his old days in the FBI, it's better not to say anything if you really want somebody to talk.

"I mean, I know that's wrong, Scotty. But they're tearing our family apart. My sister's been crying practically nonstop since she heard the news, and Dad's walking around like a zombie."

"What's he saying?"

"That it's all his fault."

"And is it? All of it?"

"Yes. She wouldn't be leaving if he wasn't a drunk. And she'd take me with her, but she's trying to leave it to me because I'm old enough to make my own decisions about life now. I'm sure that's what she's thinking." He starts picking at blades of grass. "I know. I mean, I can't blame her for feeling like this wasn't the life she signed up for."

"No. I guess not. Did she realize he was a drinker?"

"I don't know. Her dad was an alcoholic. I can't imagine she didn't see the signs in Dad. He's been drinking ever since I was old enough to notice."

"I doubt she'd have married him knowing that. I mean, with her dad being an alcoholic. At least she has you, Angus."

"She's been there for me. She kept us going with our Scottish stuff too, homeschool, all of that."

"Not to mention the campground."

"That's true. Oh, man! I don't even know how I feel. I'm just mad. At both of them really."

"Your mom loves you, Angus, doesn't she?"

"Yeah. She does."

I start picking at grass too. "What's she going to do now?"

"She's already got a job as a secretary in Richmond at the university there, and she can get tuition credits and go back to school. She's moving in with a friend from high school who's also divorced."

"Is there anyone you can really talk to about all this? Somebody who truly understands?"

"No. But I wish there was somebody around who really gets it."

"I'm sorry I can't."

"Don't be. That's good for you. You seem like you have such

a cool life."

That's what everybody seems to think. "It's not all it's cracked up to be."

"Yeah right." He huffs out a very cynical laugh.

Can I trust him with the truth of my life?

"Maybe you're right." I sigh. "I know I can't say anything that will make you feel better, but I can just be around. If you need that, that is. Sometimes it's better just to know somebody's around to listen. And I've been praying."

"Don't even get me started on where I think God is these days."

I lean back on my hands. "Angus, there are things about my past and my life I can't share, and while they may not be your troubles, they're not easy things. Not at all. But God has really been there for me lately."

"Good for you."

"I know. It sounds dumb. I'm sorry."

"Well, your prayers won't hurt. Maybe you can pray for me, because I just can't do it on my own right now."

"I will." I take his hand and we sit there until the sun sits directly overhead.

"You're a good person, Scotty."

"But do you ever wonder if being good is enough? I've been thinking about that a lot lately."

"Yeah, I've thought of that."

"What are you going to major in?"

"Premed."

"Really?" Cool.

"Yeah. I see a lot of sad people, old and sick people here. I want to help them out. I mean, I understand them a little more than most young people."

"I love older people. They're my favorite group."

"Really?" His eyes light up.

"Uh-huh." I nod. "The way they're so interested in every little thing you do. The way they still think cookies are special. I don't know. Everything. And they're so lonely too, a lot of them."

"I know."

"Want to drive into town and just haunt the bookstore?"

"I'd better not. Mom's probably come home from the lawyer's office. I should be there to say good-bye."

I squeeze his hand and look directly into his blue eyes. "Angus, no kid should have to go through what you're going through."

"Yeah, Scotty. I know. I wish it wasn't happening to my family. If I could go back, even a few months, maybe I could have encouraged Dad to stop drinking. I don't know."

"You couldn't have stopped it. Angus, there wasn't anything you could have done. You've got to know that."

He releases my hand and hops up. "It just doesn't feel that way."

A hawk circles overhead.

Angus lays a hand on my shoulder. "Thanks, Scotty."

"You're welcome." I smile.

And he leans forward and kisses me on my cheek. He takes my hand and we walk back down the mountain path. My first kiss, a kiss on the cheek, yes, and all I feel is a sadness because here's a wonderful guy and he's already taken. By grief. By separation. By fear. By helplessness. And there's nothing he can do right now to make it go away. Even if he were turning to God, the pain would still be there. Angus would just have Somebody walking along beside him.

And the thought hits me. God is still walking beside Angus. Because God does as he chooses, and I can't help but believe God chooses to love Angus, to support him and help him, even if Angus himself doesn't realize it.

1:30 p.m.

The rumble of Jeremy's truck causes both Dad and me to look up from our work.

"What is it with that truck?" Dad.

"Must remind him of a Harley or something. It's just Jeremy, Dad. Always has to make an entrance."

I get up and open the door. Jeremy's getting out. "Hey, kid!"

"Hi, Jeremy. Wanna come in?"

"I was hoping you'd give me some inside info."

I jump to the ground and close the door. "Can't help you much. Charley wouldn't talk about anything last night. Went right to bed and left bright and early this morning. As usual." I sigh and cross my arms.

"I was hoping she'd tell you about our talk."

"No such luck. Wanna go get ice cream or something?"

"Sure. Hop on in."

"Let me tell Dad."

A minute later we're on our way into town. I dive right in. "So, what happened?"

"Well, I tried to scout out her feelings for Harris. He's sure sweeping her off her feet, isn't he?"

I nod. Jeremy has a great jawline, and his dark, sharp eyes look straight in front of him. "He is. He's a great guy. Know anything about him?"

He nods. "Just some. Has a reputation for having a lot of integrity."

"That's good."

"He's really rich."

"Not something Charley would care about much."

He grips the steering wheel. "No kid, you got that right."

"So if his wealth makes your manliness go all berserk, don't even go there. Charley's not that woman."

He blows out a breath. "Yeah, you know you're right."

"What else?"

"He lives pretty simply on his farm in Scotland. It's a castle and all but he employs local people and is well respected in his village and all that. It's pretty remote. I couldn't find out much."

"You were researching him?"

"You bet! If somebody's going to come along and steal Charley from me, he'd better be a stand-up guy."

"Interesting choice of words, Jeremy. You talk as if she was yours to begin with."

"Yeah, there is that."

"So what have you been waiting for all these years?"

"I don't know," he whispers. "You know what it's like when you think somebody's always gonna be there waiting for you to get your act together?"

I look out the window. We're driving by a farm and some cute calves are lying out in the field, their mamas standing nearby. "No, Jeremy. I really don't. I guess I took Charley for granted. But since I've found out the truth of my life, I don't know if I'll ever take somebody for granted again."

"Guess I was taking her for granted."

"Big time."

He looks at me. "Big time? Really, kid?"

"Jeremy, do you have any idea how much Charley was in love with you?"

He shakes his head. "Guess not. And that *was* stings a little. Do you think I've got a chance left with her?"

"I don't know. But I'll tell you this, if you don't fight for her, you're the biggest fool on the planet. I don't mean to be rude, but it's just the truth."

"Yeah, kid. Yeah."

"Now, turn this truck back around and ask Charley out. Me and ice cream are a total waste of your time."

Grinning, he tips his cowboy hat back on his head. "You got it."

He does a three-point turn in the middle of the road, kicking up dust beneath the tires. "What if she's already got a date with Harris tonight?"

"Ask for tomorrow night. How much longer do you have here?"

"Four days at the most."

I whistle. "You'd better become a regular Don Juan."

"Yeah. A regular Don Juan."

"Oh come on. You can turn on the charm when you want."

"Maybe. But Charley's a whole other class of woman."

That's the nicest thing I've heard in a long time. And you know what? Charley deserves it. She's become a whole lotta somethin' else!

9:00 p.m.

A small campfire blazing, I'm waiting in the soccer-mom chair for Harris to pull up. It was a sunset shoot, guys marching to battle and *grr!!* Or should I say, "Och, aye!"

A lot of Scottish Americans came in for the shoot today as extras. A thousand men in kilts? I am *just* sayin'!

Harris pulls up in a rental car. Nothing fancy. Good for him. "Hello there, Scotty!" he says through the open window.

"Hi, Mr. Harris. Charley's primping. Wanna come sit with me? I can't surrender the pink chair, but Charley's sky blue one sits practically the same."

"Sounds like an invitation I'm incapable of refusing."

Soon he's puffing on his pipe, the curling smoke obliterated by the darkness. "This is lovely."

"I love it here. Is it true that it's a lot like Scotland?"

"Some of it, aye. Of course way up in the Highlands it's a wee bit more barren and rugged."

"Is that where your castle is?"

He shakes his head. "No. Down closer to Galloway. In the Lowlands, a place far underrated by tourists, but we like it just fine that way."

I might as well just lay out the deal. "Okay, we've got just a couple of minutes, so here's the scoop."

"The scoop? I'm intrigued."

"First of all, are you still really interested in Charley, or are you finding this is just a set romance?"

"Definitely not just a set romance. She becomes more delightful each day."

I scrunch my brow. "Really? Really, really?" I mean Charley's great, but she's my grandmother. Delightful? I just think of her as a really sweet airhead-sort of lady, even if she is a whole other class of woman, as Jeremy calls her.

"Absolutely. She's fascinating. And she knows quite a bit about organic gardening, a sideline of mine."

"She does?"

"You'd be surprised at how intelligent the woman is, my dear." He draws in on the pipe.

Wow. How odd.

"Okay, enough small talk. You know Jeremy Winger is in town. I hear he popped in on your pub date Friday. Charley loved him for years. I mean ever since I can even remember. They go back years. High school! I am telling you they totally know each other backward and forward."

He raises his brows. "Then what's wrong with the man that he didn't seize the moment and sweep her off her feet?"

"It's complicated. Me, for one thing. I'm sure Charley hasn't told you about our crazy life, at least what made us go on the road and all."

He shakes his head. "No. She hasn't mentioned that, I'm afraid."

"So suffice it to say that Jeremy really couldn't have gone after her. Until the last six months or so. But by his own admission he has taken her for granted."

Harris lays his right ankle atop his left knee. "I believe I understand what you're saying. Jeremy Winger has at long last decided to try and woo the lovely Charley Dawn."

"Bingo!" Bingo? Where the heck did that word come from? "But more importantly, I want Charley to be happy. And if it's you she's destined to be with, who she'll be most happy with, I want her to have that chance. Jeremy will only be around for the next four days. And this shoot lasts, what, another two weeks?"

"Aye. So you're saying that if I want to be in the running for your grandmother's heart, I need to draw my sword and fight like there's no tomorrow?"

"Pretty much."

He chuckles. "You're an amusing lass. But I like you."

"I like you too."

"You must if you're warning me like this."

I curl my hands around the ends of the chair arms and raise myself a little. "I also want you to know what you're up against. Jeremy is a human bulldog."

His eyes sparkle as he whispers. "Well, we'll just have to see what happens to a bulldog when faced with a lion."

I clap my hands. "I'd like to see that myself."

Charley emerges and, well, I have to admit it, in the firelight she's breathtaking. (There's that word again!) She's wearing a pale green circle skirt, a black turtleneck, and a poncho. She holds up a foot encased in one of my black leather high-heeled boots. "I didn't think you'd mind, baby."

"Of course not. Have fun you two."

"I need to be back by eleven thirty. An old friend is in town and he wants to see me."

Harris puts his arm around Charley's shoulders. "Scotty gave me the full story, dearie."

"Oh, my." She turns to me. "You really didn't. Tell me you didn't."

"What can I say, Charley? I'm honest to a fault."

She turns to Harris, ready for heartbreak. I can see it by the fear in her eyes and the sudden hunch of her shoulders. "She told you why Jeremy's here?"

"Aye. And all I can say is may the best man win!"

Me too, Harris. Me too!

He offers Charley his arm. She takes it and they walk toward his car. As he helps her in, he leans forward and whispers something. Her laughter rings like a bell.

I've never, ever heard my grandmother laugh like that before.

One hour later

"I'm so torn." I sit down on the couch. Dad's doing as promised, burning the midnight oil.

"What about, honey?" He takes off his reading glasses and squeezes the bridge of his nose.

"Charley. And Harris. And Jeremy. A month ago, I would have been so happy Jeremy was coming to woo her. And I still am. But now Harris is around and I like him too! Poor Charley!"

Dad cracks up. And as he sits there laughing, his shoulders shaking, I have to join him. Poor Charley? She's got a famous actor and an esteemed director both trying to win her heart.

"Yeah," I say. "Pretty horrible place to be in."

He holds up his hands. "I'm just sayin'."

"Are you mocking me?"

"Just a little."

"I like it."

Hollywood Nobody: May 8

Well, Nobodies, I decided to put a different spin on the blog this week! How about news about people who are getting it right for a change? Wouldn't that be a novelty in the world of Hollywood blogdom?

Today's Raves: Bono. Nuff said, right? He's a really hot, talented guy, and he cares about issues of poverty. His ONE Campaign is 2.5 million strong. Check it out here.

Audrey Hepburn. The late actress who played Holly Golightly in the classic pic *Breakfast at Tiffany's* used her status for humanitarian purposes long before it became fashionable. And she was gorgeous to boot!

Today's Quote: "You can't find any true closeness in Hollywood, because everybody does the fake closeness so well." Carrie Fisher

Okay, so the quote was a little cynical. But it's just so true!

Later!

Man, am I going to get bad comments from this blog. But I don't even care anymore. Maybe I'm just not cut out for this sort of thing. I'm not as voyeuristic as I thought. Being so caught up in the lives of celebrities just brings me down. I don't know how much longer I've got it in me to post on this thing.

Oh, an e-mail came in.

From Violette Dillinger.

Scotty,

What's happening to the blog lately, babe? Haven't seen my name in a week. Do I need a new Violette Central? No hard feelings, right?

Vi

Hey, Violette,

Just feeling a little disillusioned by the whole thing and I don't think it's going away anytime soon. Might want to rethink me as your sole connection on the Net. Want me to design you your own website? I'll maintain it and I know the Nobodies will be glad to head on over.

Scotty

Hopefully she's still online. Sure enough, a return e-mail pops into my in-box two minutes later.

Great idea! How soon can you get it done?

How about two weeks tops?

Perfect! See ya later. I'm off to the studio. Album no. 2 is almost done!

Very cool. I'll give you daily updates on the website's progress.

So here's the thing. Violette totally doesn't have to trust me with this project. She can afford top-notch Web design. But she's going to put it in my hands anyway. As I've always suspected, Violette is the real deal.

I've sure got my work cut out for me!

I call down from the loft to Dad. "I've just taken on the job of designing Violette Dillinger's new website."

He looks up. "Can you do it?"

"Sure." I don't even believe my own bravado.

"Honey . . ."

"Hey, I'm a smart chicka. I'll figure it out."

He scratches his cheek. "You know, I believe you."

A while later

A knock on the RV door.

I open it. Angus stands outside. "You got a couple of minutes?"

"Sure."

I jump down. "What's up?"

"I'm heading to my aunt's house in Kentucky for a couple of days, and then our pipe band is going to compete at KSW."

"KSW?"

"Kentucky Scottish Weekend."

"That sounds fun."

He nods. "Yeah, it is. I just wanted to say good-bye, so you didn't think I just disappeared on you."

"I appreciate that. I would have been a little worried with all that's going on."

"I know." He reaches out and takes my hand. "Thanks for being around."

"I haven't been much help."

He squeezes my hand. "Yes you have. I've needed somebody to talk to."

"I get that."

"So, I'm coming back Sunday night. Will you still be around?"

"I sure will."

"Then how about that trip to the bookstore on Monday?"

"You got it." I smile. He still hasn't let go of my hand.

"You look pretty today, Scotty." And he blushes. Man, he is just so cute.

"Thanks. Be careful. And do well. I know you will."

"I'll try. The good thing is, in bagpipes, if you forget what note comes next, you just play a G."

"What?"

"It's the tone of the drone. Sorry, I got a little Scottish geeky on you."

"I like it."

"I'd better go. Hey, can I have your cell phone number?"

"Sure." I rattle it off and he plugs it in into the address book of his phone.

"Quick. How's your dad?"

He shrugs. "Not great. Drinking more than ever. My sister's going to have to run the camp herself this weekend. She was going to compete at KSW, but with the shoot going on, there's no way we can leave it all in Dad's incapable hands."

"Oh, man."

"Yeah. Anyway, I gotta go. It's a good ways away."

"Okay."

He leans forward and looks to be going for my cheek again. But I turn my head and his kiss lands on the corner of my mouth. He pulls back and smiles. "Take care." And hops into his Jeep. He throws the shift into first and rolls off our campsite.

I watch him until he's out of sight.

4:45 p.m.

I shut my science book, power down the laptop, and grab a book *I* want to read, not my professor at IUHS. That *Lady Oracle* is bringing me down!

So, whom should I happen to grab but my fave, F. Scott Fitzgerald, my faux namesake. *The Love of the Last Tycoon*. The bummer about this book that I know up front is that he died before he finished it. But there you go. It's the last book of his for me to read, and read it I must!

I have only an hour of daylight left, so I grab the soccer-mom chair and head toward the pool. I love special haunts. A girl needs her quiet places, and when you live in an RV with your relatives, those are few and far between.

Opening my chair, I look up at the mellowing sky and allow myself to think about my mother. I sit down. I feel so connected to her now when I read Fitzgerald, and I wonder if that's one of the few connections we'll ever share.

Dad's getting his hopes up that she's still alive. He felt for years that she wasn't, and then I went and got things going again. Have I done him a grave disservice? What if she's dead?

But it's always better to know for sure, isn't it?

I'll just have to trust that it is.

My cell phone rings. Seth's dad!

"Hi, Mr. Haas."

"Scotty. I just thought you'd like to know that Edie's taken a turn for the worse. The fever was caused by pneumonia."

"Oh no!"

"It doesn't look good."

"Have you been able to contact Seth?"

"No. I think something must be wrong with his phone. Do you know what production company he's with?"

"No, but I can find out. I'll get in touch with him, Mr. Haas. You're near DC, right? What hospital are you at?"

"Fairfax General."

"Okay. Leave it to me."

"Scotty, thanks." His voice drains off. "I really appreciate you."

"Mr. Haas, if there's anything else I can do . . ."

"No. That will be more than enough. I had a bad feeling when they admitted her."

"Don't say that. Please. She'll be all right."

"I wish I could believe you."

"Is there family around?"

"No. They're all on the West Coast. Of course if the unthinkable happens—"

"It won't."

"Anyway, I'd better get back in. Keep praying, Scotty."

"I will. Tell Mrs. Haas how much I love her and that she's just got to pull through."

"When she wakes up, I'll do just that."

We ring off.

Okay, okay. I should probably head back to the TrailMama and do some serious online research. I have no idea how I'm going to find this stuff out.

Harris!

I'll bet he's got connections to everyone.

Leaving soccer mom and F. Scott at the bottom of the pool, I hightail it over to the shoot. Jumping up into Charley's kitchen trailer, I'm relieved to see her there making more of those hard biscuits.

"This is the most boring job I've ever taken." She blows her bangs out of her eyes. "Bar none."

"Charley, I've got to find Mr. Harris. Do you know where he is?"

"He's getting changed in wardrobe."

"Is he putting his costume on or taking it off?"

"Off. We're heading to town for some kind of a surprise, a romantic date. I have no idea what he's got up his sleeve. Why do you need to see him?"

I tell her.

"Go ahead, baby. I think you're right. If anybody can find Seth it'll be Tony."

Tony? So he's Tony now? Well, well.

I ask some British soldier for directions to wardrobe, and he points the way. I pray I won't run into Evans.

I don't. Thank you, God, for the little things. I push my way past ladies in peasanty clothing and guys splashed with fake blood, and a couple of noble looking men, and Liam Neeson who says, "Hello there!"

I wave and say, "Hi, Mr. Neeson!" and run right on by.

Fame schmame.

I'm just sayin'.

Harris emerges from one of the trailers. Wearing blue jeans and a sweater, he looks handsome, in a regular-guy way. "Mr. Harris!"

"Scotty!"

I rush up. "I'm so glad I found you." Wooh. I've got to catch my breath.

"What's the matter? Is your grandmother all right?"

"Yes. But I need to ask you a favor."

"Well if it'll help my cause, gladly."

I take his arm and pull him to a less populated spot. I explain the situation.

"Let me call my agent. He's quite in the know."

I nod.

Harris dials, explains the situation, does a little gentlemanly coercing, and hangs up. "Give him five minutes."

"Okay. Phew! Okay. So tell me about the big date tonight and I promise I won't spill the beans."

"Oh I trust you, lovey. We're going to the symphony hall. I've hired half the Asheville Symphony Orchestra to serenade us while we have a picnic dinner on stage."

"Oh no!" I gasp, bringing my hands up to my mouth. "You can't do that!"

"Why ever not?"

"It's not even close to Charley's style. She's a walk-on-the-beach, tea-on-the-porch kind of person, Mr. Harris. She won't be impressed by your grandeur, she'll be impressed by the fact that you are, underneath all the Hollywood hype, a good man who enjoys the simple things in life."

"Oh, dear."

"You might want to give the orchestra the night off."

He starts dialing and gets the director on the line. "It's off. You'll all still be paid, of course, but it's off. Thank you very much." And he doesn't stay on the line for more information than that. "You saved the day, Scotty."

"Thanks. I try."

He laughs. His phone rings. He answers, listens, then says, "Aye, Stanley, thanks, then." Pocketing the phone, he nods. "Laughing Owl Productions. He's texting me the number that will go straight to the director."

"Wow. Okay, one more favor— "

"Aye, Scotty, I'll make the call for you."

Five minutes and a zillion transfers later, Harris gives the message and is assured Seth will receive it.

"Thank you so much!" I throw my arms around him and he smells so good. A lot better than Jeremy, to tell you the truth.

He gives me a quick squeeze and lets me go. "I'm trusting you'll keep putting in a good word for me."

I laugh. "Like you really need me to do that."

His face drops with seriousness. "For the first time in my life, I think I do. It's strange to be in this position again. But it's a little thrilling too."

"Well if it was me picking, I'd pick you hands down, Mr. Harris. For the smell of the pipe tobacco alone."

He chuckles. "Never thought of that as an asset."

"I'd better go. Dad's fixing supper."

"Take good care of yourself, Scotty."

And I hurry away with a wave. Because I've got a big plan, you see, and it all hinges on Dad.

Wednesday, May 9

It's a no-brainer, and Dad agrees. If Seth is going to keep up this silent treatment toward his mom, I'll show up on his behalf. It won't be the same for Mrs. Haas, I know, but it's what I can do. Dad drops me off at Asheville Regional Airport for a 6:10 a.m. flight. I connect in Charlotte, spend a three-hour layover reading the dreaded *Lady Oracle*, then get into Dulles International around eleven.

The cab ride to Fairfax General costs about a million dollars but I have an interesting time talking with—according to the license displayed in the cab—Mutara Boshoso, a refugee from Rwanda. Of course I've already seen *Hotel Rwanda* and I ask if he fled that bloody conflict.

"Very terrible time. Yes. I was fourteen. Lost both my parents."

Thirteen years ago. He's only twenty-seven and he looks forty. I don't ask whether he is Hutu or Tutsi because I don't want to offend him either way.

"Do you have any brothers or sisters living?" I ask.

"I don't know. I was separated early on. I haven't seen them since the day they were taken away."

"That's awful."

"Yes it is. Have you brothers or sisters?"

"No. I have a dad, but we don't know whether my mother is alive or not."

His eyes meet mine in the rearview mirror. "Then we have some little bit in common."

"Maybe a little bit. I wouldn't presume to understand what you must have gone through."

"Is okay. Pain finds itself all over the world, little miss."

Little miss. His endearment warms my heart.

I look out the window as the DC suburbs whiz by. What a miserable place. I'm sure it's better farther in. Or maybe not.

"Do you like it here in DC?"

He nods. "I have a wife now and I'm at university. We're doing what we can to make a good life."

"That's good."

"And why are you headed to hospital? Family there?"

"Sort of. Good people who've befriended me. The mother has cancer and she's not doing too well."

"Then you have my prayers."

"Thank you. Do you pray a lot?"

I mean, I'm not going to pass up the chance to find out why a person who's experienced so much horror still has faith enough to pray.

"Yes. Many times a day. God hears me. I cannot say that I always understand his ways. But here I am, with a family, and he provides for us. I have not been hungry or in danger for many years now."

"And that's saying something as a DC cab driver!"

He laughs. A deep, resounding "Ha! Ha! Ha! You got a good point."

"But why does he protect some people and not others?"

"Little miss, when you find out the answer to that, you come find me. I should like to know that too."

"But you still have faith?"

"I do. God's never lost faith in me, why should I lose faith in him?"

So Mutara tells me all about his children and his wife, a refugee from Sierra Leone, and the life they are building. "You must go on," he finally says as he pulls up to the hospital, "because as long as there is life for you, there is hope for you. You understand, little miss?"

I nod. "I think I do."

"And you go and give great hope and love to your woman friend inside there."

I reach forward and pay the cab fare and his warm brown fingers touch mine, giving me the courage I need to be with the Haases at such a terrible time. "I will, sir. Thank you so much. You've been really nice."

"Ah, yes. God bless you, my friend."

And I walk into the hospital lobby thinking, *God does, Mutara. You know, he really does.*

Fifteen minutes later

Mr. Haas almost looks like he's seen a ghost when I walk into the hospital room and say, "Surprise!"

"Scotty! Well, this is a surprise!" He turns to his wife. "Edie, look, Scotty's here."

"I see." She coughs, a wracking sound that seems to vibrate her entire body. "Oh, my. That wears me out."

"How are you doing?"

"A little better today." She smiles. A weak smile. She looks just like herself, only smaller and paler and with IVs snaking out of her hand and an oxygen tube under her nose.

"The doctor said her fever is down from yesterday. Just a touch, but we'll take what we can get, right, Edie?"

She nods. "I'm very tired. But Scotty, I'm so glad you've come."

"Why don't you rest a little bit? Scotty and I will leave you in peace so we can catch up and you can rest."

"Only if you'll repeat your conversation later on."

"Promise," I say.

"So how is she really?" I put my arm through Mr. Haas's as he walks me down the hall.

"Her fever is barely down. They have her on a heavy round of antibiotics. You saw the oxygen."

"I hate to ask this but—"

"Yes, there's always the chance we could lose her. She's already so weakened from the chemo."

"Oh, Mr. Haas."

He lays his hand atop my arm and squeezes. He's going to be strong right now. I know it and I can only hope there's somebody in his life he can lean on. Not Seth obviously! But it's also not an almost-seventeen-year-old girl, no matter how supportive she's trying to be.

"We're all praying, the people at church too. God's healed people of far graver illnesses."

But what if he doesn't this time?

"Mr. Haas, God hasn't given up on Mrs. Haas, so I guess we'd best not give up on him."

"Exactly."

Thanks, Mutara.

Two hours later

Mrs. Haas has just awakened from her nap, and Mr. Haas and I are watching an old rerun of *The Joker's Wild* when Seth walks into the room. Oh good. He came!

Karissa walks into the room. I don't believe this.

I step away from the bedside, and Seth rushes over, the Karissa right behind him. I grab her arm and pull her next to me. I whisper as softly as I can, "This is so not about you."

Mr. Haas comes to my rescue. "I need a cup of coffee. Why don't you come down to the cafeteria with me, Karissa? I'm sure you could use one too after your early flight."

"Okay." Karissa nods, surprisingly enough. They disappear from the room and I watch as Mrs. Haas, struggling for breath, tells Seth how glad she is he came.

"Mom, I'm sorry."

"Scotty told us your cell phone probably stopped working."

He looks at me with a nod of gratitude. I look at him, breathing in through my nose and trying to hide my disdain, which longs to burst all over the room like the mother of all sneezes.

"Cell phones are so cheap these days." He looks back to me.

"Scotty, do you mind if I spend some time alone with Mom?"

"No problem. I'll be right outside."

In the hallway I fume. The petty part of me wants to tell Mrs. Haas the truth, if she didn't see it herself with Seth bringing the Karissa along, but what good would it do? She deserves to be happy right now.

I sit in the waiting area across the hall wondering how someone with such a great mom could so take her for granted. Doesn't he realize what he has? Doesn't he see he's throwing away the best thing in his life for a sleazy starlet who's going to pitch him by the wayside when a better deal comes along? He won't always be Seth Hot.

Her time will end too, for that matter. But that's beside the point.

A few minutes later, Karissa and Mr. Haas return. They stop in front of me.

"Seth wanted to be alone with Mrs. Haas," I say.

"I think I'll head back in." Mr. Haas goes back into the room.

Karissa takes a step forward. "I'll— "

"Come sit here with me."

She stares me down. Or tries to.

"I'm serious. Let them be together as a family."

"Yeah, I guess."

She sits down, leaving a seat between us. Silence thickens like school paste until she turns to me. "Just so we're clear, Seth brought me here for a reason. If you know what I mean."

I roll my eyes. "Karissa, cut the crap. Nobody wants you here except for Seth. His parents don't like you, and of course you know exactly how I feel about you."

"As if I care."

"Number one, 'as if I care' was last used in 1997. And number two, what you and Seth do in your private moments just grosses us out. Not to mention that if sex is the only reason Seth brought you along, you must have little else to offer."

"Humph . . . whatever."

I give her the little *w* sign. "Are you going to call me a *loser* next?"

"You're just jealous of me."

"Yes, Karissa. I'm jealous because your life seems to be turning out so well."

"I'm done talking to you."

"I'm not the one who started this conversation."

She flips her hair and picks up a magazine on the coffee table. There they are on the cover, the glory that is . . . the Splat Pack. *Underage Drinking a Real Problem with Hollywood's Hottest Youth* the headline blares.

Well, at least there's the "hottest" part.

Karissa quickly folds back the cover.

I pull F. Scott Fitzgerald out of my backpack. So there.

Thirty minutes later

Seth shuffles out of the room, hands deep in his pockets. "Wow," he whispers. "I had no idea she was so sick."

The Karissa hops to her feet. "Oh, baby, you couldn't have known."

I stand up. "We've got to talk, Seth."

"We are talking."

"Are you sure you want me to say this here?"

He folds his arms across his chest. "Go right ahead."

Okay then, here goes. "I'm ap*palled* at the way you've been acting. You're disgusting, Seth Haas. This is your mother, Seth. Your mother. She raised you. And she is a good mom. And I covered for you. So I don't feel bad laying this out for you at all. Your mom called me looking for you. Your dad called me looking for you. He called again when he still hadn't heard from you and told me your mom was in the hospital. And even though I texted you, you never got in touch with them. I know your phone wasn't broken. So what was so important that you'd do this to your parents?"

Karissa says, "I don't think you're being fair. You have no idea what kind of pressure Seth was— "

Seth lays a hand on her arm. "Karissa, you need to go get another cup of coffee."

"You don't need to tell me what to do."

His jaw muscle clenches. "Then we'll go somewhere else. Come on, Scotty. Let's get some coffee."

Okay, this is different from any Hollywood script I've ever read. But good. I grab the tabloid off the coffee table and follow him. It's amazing, but the Karissa stays put by the hospital room.

We round the corner to the canteen area where several vending machines offer less than stellar choices, but who cares. Seth pulls out a chair for me at one of the small tables and we both sit down.

"You didn't have to lay all that on me in front of Karissa."

"I gave you a choice, Seth. And was anything I said not true?"

"Even if it was true, this is none of your business. You think you've become part of this family, but the truth of the matter is, Scotty, you're nobody."

I'll let that remark sting later. "Better a nobody who cares about the people she loves than a big somebody who won't even call his mother when she's dying of cancer. So you can call me a nobody all you want, Seth"—his eyes start to well up—"but I came without being begged, without a friend having to move heaven and earth to find me, and at the end of the day, that matters more than any name you'll ever call me."

"You—"

I hold up my hand. "I'm not finished. Would you have ignored your mom a year ago?"

He shakes his head.

"When I met you, you were one of the nicest guys I'd ever met. You were nice to a fifteen-year-old who had never made a friend in the world. We ate cheeseburgers, you helped me with my math, you introduced me to your parents"—I whip out the tabloid, holding up the cover to his face—"and look at you now. The leader of the Splat Pack. Please tell me a part of the Seth Haas I knew back on Ocracoke is still down in there somewhere."

He rests his elbows on the table and cradles his forehead in his palms. "It all happened so fast," he whispers.

I stay silent.

And Seth's shoulders start to shake. "What's happening to me?"

4:00 p.m.

Thank goodness Seth sent the Karissa to whatever hotel it is they're staying at.

I've been sitting here all afternoon reading quietly. The hospital has Wi-Fi, so I dig my laptop out of my backpack and check my e-mail.

Grampie!

Scotty Dear,

I wanted you to be the first to know. Grammie and I found a great home in Delaware half a block from the beach! It's got four bedrooms — one of which is yours, my dear — a roomy kitchen and a great room with a stone fireplace. Are you seeing a family making s'mores, because I am! And in the back, a small in-ground pool, in case you don't want to make the walk to the beach.

One of the bedrooms is on the main floor for Grammie and myself, because we're getting to be old coots. Here's the link at the realtor's website so you can see for yourself. We'll be hanging around the area in the Beaver Marquis for the next couple of weeks until closing, at which time, Asheville, here we come. If you'll have us.

Grammie says she loves you, as do I. Give your dad and Charley our love too.

Grampie

I write back right away. Of course. A big smile on my face.

"What's the big news?" Seth asks.

"Grammie and Grampie are buying a new house in Delaware. Near the beach. So the Dawn clan will have a place to come home to."

Of course, Seth knows the whole scoop about our family now. So, probably, do his parents, and wouldn't the FBI have a field day with that?

"Very cool, Scotty. That must mean a lot to you guys."

"You have no idea."

"Yeah," he whispers. "You're right about that. At least I didn't. Man." He shakes his head. "Where are you staying tonight?"

"I'm flying back on the red-eye."

"We rented a car. I'll drive you back to the airport."

"I'd appreciate it. How long are you staying?"

"Until tomorrow."

"You should know more by then."

He nods. "Let's hope she improves a lot."

"For her sake or yours?"

"For hers."

"You mean that, Seth?"

"Yeah, Scotty. I really do."

11:00 p.m.

We pull up to the great cement sculpture that is Dulles Airport.

"Scotty, I'm sorry for what I said. About you being a nobody."

"That was Karissa talking."

He nods. "Maybe. But I said it, and I'll take the blame. You're the last person I want to hurt."

"Really?"

"Uh-huh. Man, I've just been so caught up in everything. People wanting to be around me. And I've got offers for films for the next five years if I want them."

"It must be pretty dazzling."

He raps the steering wheel. "That's it. Although *blinding* might describe it more accurately."

I shrug. "Seth, it was your first year in Hollywood. I guess it's to be expected."

"I thought there was more to me."

I turn in the seat, leaning my back against the door. "There is more to you. It's not too late to turn back around."

"Leave my career behind?"

"No. No, you're too good on camera. But it's possible to have this career and live a halfway decent life." I give him a slanty smile.

He returns the favor. "I don't know what I'm going to do about Karissa."

"Do you love her, Seth? I mean, really?"

"No. But we've just done so much—"

I jam my palms against my ears. "No, no, no! No oversharing! I do not want to hear it!"

He laughs. "Okay. Sorry."

"Seth, you can't tie yourself down to her because you've made mistakes. And maybe"—I bap him on the shoulder—"you're assuming too many feelings on her part. Has she told you she loves you?"

"No."

"So that's good, right?"

"Well, yes. I guess it is."

"Are you going to break up with her?"

He sighs. "I've got to. She brings out the worst in me."

"Hallelujah!" I yell.

"What are you talking about?"

"You've finally seen the light, Seth Haas. And pardon me for saying so, but it took you long enough."

He reaches out to give me a hug. "You still my little sis?"

Oh brother. Not that again! "Of course. I'll always be." I pull back. "And hey, I've got a sort-of boyfriend now."

"You do?"

You could scrape the poor lad, as Harris would call him, up off the floor of the car.

"Yeah. I met him on the movie set. He's a bagpiper named Angus."

"How old is he?"

"Eighteen. Just."

"Just? Are you sure?"

"Yes, Seth, I'm sure."

"Because, Scotty, if he's a jerk to you, just say the word and I'll—"

"What? Give him lessons on how to take it to the next level?"

"I deserve that."

"Yes. But from here on out, let's pretend everything's always been good, and let's make sure it always will be."

"You got it."

1:10 a.m.

In Charlotte, I find my seat on the plane for leg two of my return trip. A young woman sits in the seat next to mine. She smiles sweetly and gets out because I've got the window seat.

"I'm sorry." I shove my backpack beneath the seat in front of me.

"Oh, sheesh, no prob!" She waves a friendly hand, her white, gauzy angel sleeve swinging around her narrow wrist. "Planes make everybody nervous."

"I know." I sit down.

So does she. "I'm Megan, by the way."

"Scotty."

"Cute name. You live in Asheville?"

"Nope. Just passing through with my family."

"Cool."

"What about you?"

She leans forward and pulls a spiral notebook out of her army green rucksack. "I'm from there. Going home for a few days, then I'll head back to work."

Megan's pretty in that ballet-dancer sort of way. Her dark hair is pulled severely back from her fine-boned face. She's got a swipe of gloss on her full lips and some liner drawn around her dark eyes. In this light it's hard to tell what color they are.

"What do you do?" I ask.

"I'm a missionary."

"No kidding! You don't look like a missionary." Well, that just sort of popped out!

"Well, you've got me there, if you expect an old lady in orthopedic shoes."

I laugh. "To tell you the truth. I don't know what I expected a missionary to look like. It's not like I've ever met one before. I just didn't expect one to look like you."

"Disappointed?"

"No. I think it's cool. So what do you do? Do you live in Africa or something?"

She slips a pen out of the rucksack next. "Contrary to popular opinion, we don't all wind up in Africa, not that it's a bad place to end up, mind you."

"Then where are you stationed?" Okay, I think *stationed* must be the wrong word. But I don't know this lingo . . . at all.

"I'm in Appalachia. Eastern Kentucky." She begins to doodle on the page.

"Cool. You can stay here in the U.S. and it still counts as being a missionary? I had no idea."

She cocks her head. "I'm taking it you haven't been in church much."

"No. I'd like to be. But, well, my life's complicated. We're on the road for my grandmother's job, so we're never in one place for long." I look over at her notebook. She's drawing groovy flowers.

"That's a shame."

"Yeah. I'm kinda used to it." But soon, there'll be Grammie and Grampie's house!

"So anyway, yes, it counts if it's over here too. There's a lot of poverty in the region. I work at an orphanage."

"Really? There are still orphanages?"

She looks shocked and I deserve to have her say, "Where have you been all your life?" but she's way too gentle to do that. "There are. You can imagine there are a lot of illegitimate births, and our home, well, it's for the kids whose families are too poor to take care of them. It's really sad."

"Wow. It must be hard."

She nods. "It's not for everyone to serve Christ this way."

I perk up. "So you do this because you're a Christian?"

"Uh-huh. Pure and simple."

I unzip my backpack. "I'm sure there's nothing simple about it."

"Oh, but it's very simple. Can I share a Bible verse with you?"

"Well, you're a missionary, aren't you? I mean isn't that part of what you do?"

"Yeah." She wrinkles up her nose. "I can definitely get away with the Bible stuff more than most people."

"I like it."

Relief washes over her features. "Really?"

I nod. "Most definitely. I have a lot of questions about my faith. My grandmother doesn't want to hear about that sort of thing. My Dad has faith, and he answers when I ask, but otherwise he's quiet about it."

"Okay." She digs into her pack and pulls out a tiny green Bible that fits into the palm of her hand.

"That's so cool! Where did you get that?"

"The American Bible Society."

"Who are they?"

"I'll get to that later if you'd like. Anyway, here's the verse." She quickly flips to the sought-after passage. She must know her stuff. Pointing to the verse with her index finger, she says, "James 1:27, right there. Go ahead and read it."

The fine print doesn't elude me. I get that warm sensation as I whisper the words, "'Religion that God our Father accepts as pure and faultless is this: to look after orphans and widows in their distress and to keep oneself from being polluted by the world.'"

"Exactly!" She pulls the Bible away and sets it down on her notebook.

"So you're looking after the orphans."

"Yep. That's what I do."

"I thought missionaries just went around talking about Jesus."

She shakes her head. "No, we do that. But we do lots of other things. It's amazing how telling people about God's love makes so much more sense when you're doing the pure-religion stuff along with it."

"Makes sense. And the being-polluted-by-the-world stuff?"

"Equally as important. Gives us moral credibility. I mean who's going to believe Jesus has better things for them if the person delivering the message can't stop sleeping around or taking drugs or whatever?"

"That makes sense too."

"It's called personal holiness."

"John Wesley!"

"You know of him?"

"I love that guy," I say.

She opens her notebook to the pocket in the cover and pulls out a card. "Here's my card. I've got e-mail and stuff, so if you ever want to ask me any of those questions, well, I can get pretty lonely, so I'll be glad to answer them."

"Thanks!"

I pull out my own Bible and tuck it in the pages.

"So you've got a Bible."

"Not a cool little green one."

"Here." She places it in my hands. A New Testament. "Take this. I've got another one at home."

"Are you sure?"

"Positive."

I tuck it in my backpack.

The stewardess does her thing, explaining the exits, scaring the pants off of anybody who has an ounce of latent fear lurking inside of them.

Soon enough, we're in the air, kudos to the captain, and Megan turns toward me again. "So we've got fifty minutes for you to ask me questions, and I promise you that I might not have the answers!" She laughs.

I join in. "Well, that's okay. So, it's like this: I started on this faith thing, like full-fledged—"

"What do you mean by full-fledged?"

"I was wondering about Jesus and all before then. But then I had this experience where I knew I needed him. Does that make sense?"

"Sure."

"So, now that he's part of my life, I want him to be a bigger part. I read my Bible and pray, but there's got to be way more to it than that. Or at least that's what I think."

"I agree."

"The problem is, I don't know what else to look for, to attain to."

"Well, the first step is to try to be like Jesus."

"So how do I try and do that?"

"Read the gospel books. Matthew, Mark, Luke, and John. And while you're doing it, pay close attention to everything Jesus said, and what he did. Have you read the gospels?"

I nod. "Yeah. But I could do it again, I'm sure."

"So you know Jesus was all about helping people not only get closer to God, his Father, but about healing them, feeding them, hanging out with them."

"That's true."

"So it may stand to reason that because he did all those things for people, his words about his Father rang truer than if he hadn't cared about them personally."

Yeah. I get that. "Wow."

"So do that, and as you read, e-mail me and let me know your thoughts."

"I will!"

So then we start talking about my life, which she thinks is cool. Her life, which is even cooler. And before I want it to, the plane lands in Asheville.

She gives me a hug after we head outside and then runs toward her parents. A chubby woman in a pantsuit and a man in an Adidas athletic outfit and big white sneakers.

I hug my biker-looking Dad.

"I'm glad you're back, honey."

"Thanks, Dad. Sorry it's so late."

"Hey, I was burning the midnight oil anyway."

True. True.

Thursday, May 10

I log onto my e-mail this morning to over four hundred comments about how lame my blog is. But instead of responding, I get through my schoolwork as quickly as possible and set to designing Violette's website. After a quick back and forth on IM, she says she wants a clean, simple, serious-artsy look with just a bit of whimsy. I suggest . . . violets. She said, "Oh, yeah."

So there you have it. Dark gray with some violets. Some brooding black and white pictures because her new album has no trace of bubblegum flavor. This, I can do.

Dad refills my coffee and suggests some mac 'n' cheese for lunch, and by twelve thirty, I'm back in my loft working on the site. My phone buzzes. Text message. Angus.

Angus: I'm in Kentucky. You doing okay?

Oh joy! A complete-word texter. Like me.

Me: Fine. I'm getting a lot of school done. How's your aunt?

Angus: Really angry at my dad. She's my mom's sister.

Me: Must be nice to have a sympathetic, outside ear.

Angus: Yeah. Although it kind of makes me feel sorry for Dad!

Me: Is that good?

Angus: Who knows? So I'll be out of touch for the next couple of days. Lots of practice and setting up. She's on the board of the festival.

Me: I'll keep the spot on the hill warm for you.

Angus: Thanks. Take care.

Me: You too. And be good!

Angus: Ha. Ha. I'll try.

So that was pretty cool. Just checking in and all that. Which means he was thinking about me. You *know* I like that!

Four hours later

Charley stands at the edge of the pool. "Baby, what are you doing here? When I asked . . . Ezra . . . where you were, he told me here and I couldn't believe it. Are you okay?"

"Charley, sitting at the bottom of a swimming pool is okay if it's empty. It's just a cool place."

"Groovy. Okay"—she starts down the steps—"I really need your help."

I set aside the *Tycoon*. "What's up?"

"Yesterday was amazing."

"I'm assuming you're talking about the latest show here at the campground, *Win Charley's Heart*."

"Uh-huh. Yesterday, I came to the trailer and it was full of flowers."

"Cool! What kind?"

"Roses, at least ten dozen of them, from Jeremy."

"Whoa, Jeremy."

"And then all these bouquets from Tony. Flowers from around here. And he tied them all with different-color ribbons and each one had a card with a poem he handwrote on them."

The man obviously listens to advice. "Poems he wrote?"

"Some. Others were 'my love is like a red red rose' and stuff."

"Ironic choice considering Jeremy's blooms. Kinda brought

all those into his fold."

"I know. So then right after I got off work, Jeremy took me out for a candlelit dinner at a French restaurant in town, and he talked about wasted years and really laid out his feelings. And we had such a good time remembering the past years and I thought about how much we've been through together, how he was always there for us, always did what he could to protect us, to do for you what he could."

"That's true. Jeremy's always been there."

"And then Tony took me up for dessert under the stars. And get this, he made a pie himself. It was the ugliest pie I've ever seen, baby!" She laughs.

I do too. "Oh, Charley! But did it taste good?"

"No! It tasted as bad as it looked. But it was the sweetest thing I've ever put in my mouth. And he held my hand, and . . . well, he kissed me. Just a sweet little kiss on the lips and I felt so cherished. It's like he laid his eyes on me once and saw me for me."

"That's true too. You really are in a pickle aren't you?"

"Yes!"

"Do you love either of them?"

She throws her weight on her left foot and crosses her arms. "I think I'm falling in love with Tony."

"Wow." I get up and let her have the soccer-mom chair.

"I know." She sits down and blows out a sigh of relief. "Oh that feels good. I've been on my feet all day."

It always amazes me her ankles don't swell to the size of hams.

"Anyway, but with Jeremy, well, I love him. I can't say it's the romantic love I feel for Tony. But we've been through so much together, and he's such a good man."

"So how can I help?" I sit down on the concrete. Luckily it's dry. I pick up a brown, crispy leaf and go to work on it.

"I've got to decide. Jeremy's leaving the day after tomorrow, and for some reason, I really want to send him off with an answer."

"Did he say he wants to marry you?"

She nods. "Uh-huh. Isn't that crazy?"

"No, Charley. It makes perfect sense. What about Harris? What's he saying about a more permanent arrangement?"

"Nothing yet. I mean, we've only known each other for about a week. And there's no way I'm going to ask him how serious he is!"

"Well, he picked a gazillion wildflowers and baked you a pie. That says something all on its own, doesn't it?"

"It does. And I think this could turn into something permanent and wonderful. It's like we were made for each other. I told him everything about me last night, baby. All my mistakes, my failures, and he didn't even flinch. You know what he said?"

"I can't imagine." Actually I can. Harris is so cool.

"He said, 'If all that made you who are right now, then I'm thankful for it.' Isn't that amazing?"

"Wow. So what did you say to that?"

"I cried."

Charley *never* cries.

"So what do you want me to do?"

"Okay. I really trust your judgment. You know me better than anybody else does. I want you to interview them."

"*Interview* them? Are you kidding me?" Charley's come up with some pretty crazy ideas in her time, but this? Oh, man.

"I'm not kidding. Can you think up a couple of questions

for them, insightful ones that will reveal whether or not they're good for me? I just get so caught up emotionally, I can't see things clearly."

She's right about that.

"Okay. But you have to tell them it's your idea. I don't want either of them to think I'm being overprotective of you and getting all in your business. Sheesh, Charley, even you have accused me of meddling."

"You got it. So I'll give you tonight to think about the questions, and tomorrow you can talk to them."

I nod. "Can I count it for homeschool?" I laugh.

"You can count it for anything you like, baby."

"Charley, how has this shoot been?"

"Not good, baby. I don't know how much longer I can live like this. I'm tired. I'd just like a little herb garden and a cat. We've talked about a cat for so long."

Oh wow. This Harris thing is serious. Charley wants to nest and I don't blame her.

Midnight

Seth: I did it. I tld Krssa 2 go on bck to LA

Me: Good for you. How did she take it?

Seth: Nt wll. As u mght gues.

Me: I'm thinking you won't be in the Splat Pack anymore.

Seth: Its prbably a good thng.

Me: Probably?

Seth: No. ur rght. Its a good thng, but its going 2 b hrd whn I gt bck.

Me: Then don't go back. I mean, go back, do your job, get a house somewhere else, and just go back when you need to work. Lots of actors do that.

Seth: Ive burnd thru mst of my mony.

Me: What about your next film?

Seth: Ive gt th signing check comng soon.

Me: Enough for a downpayment?

Seth: Smewhre othr thn CA. yeah.

Me: How about Delaware?

Seth: Near Grmmie and Grmpie I assume.

Me: Why not?

Seth: Ill thnk about it. i wldn't be 2 far frm mom and dad there.

Me: How is your mom?

Seth: Im relievd. she took a trn 4 the btter tody. she ll prbably b out of the hsptal day aftr tmorrw.

Me: That's good news!

Seth: Dfinitly. its late and ive gt an erly cll. id bttr go.

Me: Good night.

Seth: nite.

Friday, May 11, 9:20 a.m.

Dad left on the early flight as promised. I got up with him. Made coffee while he showered, praying as much as I could that he'd be okay. His first night on the job at Mama Agnese's is tonight, and I don't care how much a man changes outwardly, somebody is sure to recognize him. And the people Dad's up against are nobody's fools.

Saturday, May 12

I'm still working on my list of questions, but I think I've got most of them. Harris is dropping by during lunch, and he said he'd bring the rest of the pie. (Oh joy.) And Jeremy's coming at three. He said I could drive his truck around the campground for some practice. (Oh joy!)

But for now, I've got to keep working on Violette's website.

12:10 p.m.

Charley was right. This is a horrible pie. Berries. All kinds mushing around in the most overly sweet syrup with lumps of flour in it, and the crust is about as tough as Jack Palance's skin, God rest his soul. I smile at Harris, trying to chew the bite as convincingly as I can, nodding, acting, acting, acting like it's the best thing I've ever eaten.

Harris nods, smug. "I was right about you, my dear. You've got acting in your blood!"

I laugh.

"It's terrible, isn't it?" he says.

"Awful."

"And your grandmother ate her entire piece and asked for another one. I spared her though."

"She's got that way about her."

Of course, Harris is smoking his pipe. "So I'm ready for the interview. I have to memorize my lines, otherwise I'd just as soon sit here wiling away the day with my favorite teenager."

"I'll bet you say that to all the teenagers in your life."

"No. You're the only one I know these days."

I blurt out a laugh. "So then, I guess the first question I have to ask you concerns me. Because I'm Charley's number-one priority. She's more like a mother to me than a grandmother."

"So I see. That's as plain as the noses on all our faces."

"How would having a wife with a teenage granddaughter-more-like-a-daughter sit in your present life plans?"

"Well, now, I've thought about that."

"Really? You've thought that far? How come?"

He puffs on his pipe and picks at the left knee of his trousers. "I've guarded my heart for years, Scotty. It's as if I always knew there was somebody else for me out there and I couldn't be too careful. When I met your grandmother, something inside me cried out. It sounds a wee bit silly at my age. But the past week, getting to know her, I find my instincts were correct."

"A few days ago, you said you didn't know where the relationship would go."

"I do now. If she'll let it."

"Wow."

"Aye. Wow is right. I'm as surprised as anybody. I thought at my age it probably wasn't going to happen again."

"So back to my question." I reach over to the picnic table and pick up the Coke he brought me.

"I think it would all work out beautifully. I'm down to one carefully selected picture a year, and I have a lot of space in Scotland. And"—he holds up his index finger—"your grandmother and I could travel over here as much as she wants to spend time with you."

"Wouldn't that get old after awhile?"

"Sometimes we do things because it's the right thing to do, Scotty dear. Whether we enjoy it or not is completely up to us. I've always been a make-the-most-of-the-situation sort of fellow."

"Good. So we'd still get to see each other a lot."

"Absolutely. And you could spend as much time in Galloway as you'd like. There's a good girls' school nearby, and we have the loveliest kirk in the village that I enjoy."

"Okay, that leads me to question two. You seem like you're a person with faith. Is that true?"

"Aye. A quiet faith, I suppose, in that I don't try to proselytize people I don't know, but a true one."

"I could tell."

"That's good to know."

"Then you know Charley's a little disappointed in God."

He nods and reaches for the mug of coffee he brought. He takes a sip, then sets it back down on the ground beside the chair.

"We've talked about it a bit. But I've got time, lass. It isn't as if we'll elope tomorrow. God will bring her to a place where she can see his love."

"You really think so?"

"Aye. You're making a great impact on her."

"Me? No way, Mr. Harris. I don't mean to be disrespectful or anything, but I can't even see how that's possible."

He shrugs. "That's what she told me."

"I think I'm still sort of a brat if you want to know the truth."

He lets out his great laugh. "Well, we'll leave that between you and God."

I look down at my list. "Next question. What about yourself makes you worry that Charley would leave you if she finds out?"

"Oh, dear! You ask the hard ones, don't you?"

"Yep!"

"I don't have a lot of skeletons in the closet. But I suppose, I'd be worried if she saw inside my heart and saw how frightened I am at times. Of the press I receive. Of what happens in the world. Of my own insignificance in the grand scheme of life."

"Is that why you live so remotely?"

"I'd have to say yes."

"Well, that's not so bad. Honestly, Charley has her own fears. She'd totally get that. I'm telling you, she's not looking for a white knight. Just a man who'll love her for who she is."

"Duly noted."

"Finally— "

"Just three questions?"

"I don't mess around."

"Clearly."

"Why do you love Charley? Do you love her? I mean, I know it's only been a short— "

"Aye, Scotty. I do love her." He gazes at the sky for a few seconds, then looks into my eyes. "She's strong. She gets her job done without complaining. She's lovely. She's raised you and done a wonderful job."

Well, thanks!

"She's a kind person. She laughs at my stupid jokes. But more than anything, she's opened herself up to me. This lovely, free spirit somehow looks at me like I was something special, and really believes it, though I don't deserve it. It's a heart connection. And when I'm not with her, Scotty, I don't feel at rest until she's within eyeshot again. Just watching her, the way she moves— "

"Okay, okay! I get it. Sheesh, Mr. Harris. You're starting to gross me out!"

That laugh again.

"So how did I do?"

"I give you an A-plus."

"Wonderful! Now how about another bite of pie?"

"Don't push your luck."

He reaches out and squeezes my shoulder. "You and your grandmother are lucky to have one another."

"It's always been her and me. And I realize she needs to move on. My dad's here now, true, but Charley and I—we're connected."

"And that's the way it should be."

"Just so we're clear." To use the words of the famed actress Karissa Bonano.

"As crystal, as they say in really poorly written films."

"Or to use the Bartholomew Evans vernacular."

"Precisely, my dear."

Harris really is my kind of guy. Having Anthony Harris for a stepgrandfather would be nothing short of amazing.

3:00 p.m.

I hop in the driver's seat of Jeremy's gargantuan truck. Dad's let me drive his little pickup before, so I'm familiar with the workings of a car, but this truck is simply ridiculous.

"I'll just stick to the campground."

Jeremy tips his hat back. "Go wherever you like, kid."

I slide the gearshift into drive and pull off our campsite. "Feels cool. Big and tough."

"You own the road now."

"I wish!" I laugh.

"So okay"—I turn toward the activities center parking lot, just to get my driving bearings—"did you ever see this day coming?"

"Being interviewed by a teenager, my entire future hanging in the balance?"

"Pretty much."

"Nope." The road is smooth enough, and nobody's coming toward me. A very good thing.

"So shoot. What questions do you have for me?"

"If you and Charley get married, what will your life look like?"

"Well, not much different, I guess. I've got a lot of projects lined up. We'll live at my ranch in Nashville when we're not on the road. But when we are on the road, we'll stay in the Airstream."

"How much are you going to be on the road this year?"

"I got backing for a new film I just wrote this past year. We'll be on location quite a bit through the summer and fall. And in January I'm doing the next leg of the big project. But by this time next year, we can settle down in Nashville for three months or so when we start editing."

"And after that?"

"Oh, you know me. I'm on the road a lot. One of those big charities is paying me to do a documentary. I'll be overseas for a couple of months."

I turn into the parking lot. "So pretty much life as usual."

"You know me, kid. Always gotta be doing something."

"Okay." I start circling around and around the center's parking lot. Now, I know I didn't ask him what he'd do with me, but that answer sounded like I wasn't even on the radar screen.

"Next question. Why do you love Charley?"

"Gee, kid. Charley's Charley, you know? I've known her almost all of my life. We've always been there for each other."

"But what about her do you love?"

"She's helped me out more than I can say. Whenever I need anything Charley's right there. She doesn't judge me or expect too much of me. She's been good to me."

I think about Harris's answer extolling the virtues of my grandmother. Other than, "She laughs at my stupid jokes and I don't deserve the way she loves me for me" stuff, pretty much everything was about Charley. Jeremy, as much as I don't want to admit it, only sees Charley as she relates to him.

In my mind, I see Charley's face as she said that Harris

appreciated her for *her* too.

"Okay then, final question. Are you pursuing Charley because you love her, really want to settle down with her, or because you don't want anybody else to have her?"

"Whoa, kid. You're not pulling any punches are you?"

"Not when we're talking about Charley."

He slides his hat back down on his brow. I circle two more times, then pull into a parking space.

"This is a really important question, Jeremy."

"No kidding."

"The fact that you have to think so long about it is about as much an answer as I need."

He shakes his head and rolls down the window, a breeze filled with the promise of rain shushing into the cab of the truck. "I don't know what I want, kid."

I grip the wheel and turn to him. "Maybe you just love Charley, Jeremy. You're attached to her because you've been friends for so long. Maybe you just don't want to lose that, so you'll try and keep it whatever way you can."

"Okay, psychologist lady."

I laugh. "But you know I could be right."

"Yeah. I'm not the settling-down type, Scotty. But I don't want to lose the closeness I feel with your grandmother."

I sigh and turn off the engine. "She deserves more than a life on the road with a man who doesn't love her like she needs."

"You're right."

I reach for his arm and grab it. "You've got to let her go. She'll always be your friend. Just not at your beck and call. That would be too much to expect from her. You know that, don't you?"

"You're right."

"You tell her though, Jeremy. Lay it all out. It'll be a clean break for her. It's what she'll need to move forward with Harris."

"I don't want to hurt her."

"Believe me, it'll be the kindest thing you can do."

Thirty minutes later

I am exhausted! Interviewing suitors is hard work.

Limeade. That'll make things better.

Retrieving the bag of limes from the fridge, I grieve a little bit. I mean, I guess we all knew this life couldn't last forever. I've thought about Charley and me separating eventually, and Dad and me striking out on our own, or better, with Babette because for some reason she's still alive. But I didn't foresee Charley finding a nice man and leaving us. It never once entered my mind.

I cut several limes in half and squeeze them as hard as I can into a tall glass, then squirt in some of the sugar syrup Dad made up for me by cooking a lot of sugar in some water until it all dissolved.

But she deserves a good life, doesn't she? I mean, she's come so far from the woman who let men walk all over her, whose own daughter wouldn't bring over her granddaughter for a visit. I crack some ice with the back of a spoon and load it in next.

I wish Dad were here. But I think I know what he'd say. That I'm right. I should tell her Harris is the way to go.

Next I pour in some tonic water.

This is too much responsibility to put on a teenager. But I'll tell her everything and see if she comes to the same conclusions I do. Because in the end, this is a decision my grandmother has to make on her own.

Then again, Jeremy might do as I ask and make my job a whole lot easier.

This is definitely the best glass of limeade I've ever made. Let's hope that's a good sign.

Yeah, I'm grasping. I just want Charley to be happy. Happier than she's ever been in her entire, disappointing life.

10:30 p.m.

I've been researching Appalachia. I hopped on the website printed on Megan's card. The Red River Home for Children. And there's Megan in the staff section, her arm around a little boy with red hair and thick glasses. He's beaming at the camera and she's beaming at him.

It's a small place. A big old house where the children are housed. Another house for babies and short-term foster care. And a center with classrooms, a cafeteria, a chapel, and an activities room.

More pictures. The Christmas play they put on last year. Sitting around a campfire. Classroom shots. Lots of shots just like the one of Megan and her fiery-haired friend.

The letter from the director, a lady named Vera Cook with very bright lipstick, tells us the story of Leah, who came with cigarette burns on her arms, so malnourished they took her to the hospital first. And there's Leah now, graduating from high school, the staff gathered around her.

"We tell these kids somebody loves them. God loves them. And here we have the opportunity to show them just how much!" she writes in the letter.

I launch my e-mail and enter Megan's address.

Dear Megan,

It's Scotty, the girl on the plane. I was just on your website. Wow. So I'm wondering if I can come visit you guys. Summer's coming soon. Need some help?

I loved meeting you. Thanks for being so nice to a stranger.

Scotty

Did I really just ask if I could come this summer? What was I thinking? What will Dad say? That was so impetuous.

Fifteen minutes later

Charley enters the TrailMama and throws her bag on the sofa. "I am so tired!"

"I'll bet." I hop down from the loft. "Want a fresh limeade?"

"That would be groovy, baby."

I repeat the process as she unwinds a coarsely woven silk scarf from around her neck.

"So what happened? Two dates tonight?"

"No. Tony's behind on memorizing his lines. He was devastated when he heard Jeremy was taking me out. Isn't that sweet?"

"He's a sweet man. I've got to admit it. So what happened with Jeremy?"

She sits at the dinette. "We had a long talk. I don't know what you said to him, but he was really honest about everything, how I needed better than him, a better life than he could provide."

"How did that make you feel?"

Charley likes those feely questions.

"A little sad, I admit." She sighs. "But he's right, Scotty. It would be more life on the road. And as he said, we all know he'll never settle down."

"What do you think about living like that?" Limes squeezed, ice cracked, I pour in the syrup.

"Can I be honest?"

"Of course."

"It sounds horrible."

I laugh. "I figured you'd think that."

"Baby, I just can't do this much longer. I'm fifty-six years old. I'm tired."

"So he let you go?"

"In so many words, uh-huh. He says he loves me, just not in the way I need him to."

"Do you think he's right?" Some tonic water next and I set the drink in front of her.

"I do."

"Me too."

Relief lightens her features. "Really?"

I nod and sit on the other side of the dinette. "You need a break, Charley. You need someone to take care of you for a change."

"Do you think Tony is the one who can?"

"Well, let's just say if he can't, I don't know who could."

"You're right about that."

"So, when are you getting together with Mr. Harris?"

"For an early breakfast."

"Are you excited?"

She nods, eyes sparkling. "I am. Baby, I don't know where things are going to go from here, but I'm ready to take a chance, ready to find out if there's something new around the corner."

"I'd say that's a good place to be."

She chugs the rest of the drink. "Let's go to bed."

"Okay. I'm tired too. And worried about Dad."

"Me too." She reaches across the table and holds my hand. "Just keep praying for him, baby."

"I'll pray for you too."

"That would be good."

Very cool. It's not like she's falling down in front of an altar or anything, but it's a start, and I'll take it.

11:32 p.m.

Dad: I'm fine. Just so you know!

Me: I was worried.

Dad: Lots to tell you. I'll be home by noon tomorrow. Make us a nice lunch.

Me: Okay! I love you so much!

Dad: I love you too, honey. Now go to bed!

Me: You too! Good night.

Dad: Good night, sleep tight, don't let the bed bugs bite.

Sunday, May 13

I'm fixing lunch, tomatoes stuffed with tuna salad, when Dad walks into the RV.

I scream with joy, throwing myself into his arms.

He twirls me around. I love this so much. I have a lot of twirling to make up for, so I don't take one episode of twirling for granted.

"So what happened?"

"Sit down. Worry about finishing lunch later."

"Okay. Is it good news?"

"Well, God must have sent some guardian angels or something. It was pretty crazy."

I slide into the dinette, and he pours himself a cup of coffee from the fresh pot I just made for him.

He takes a sip and sits down. "So I went into work Friday night. Did fine. Kept my ear to the ground hoping Robertsman wouldn't come in."

"Did he?"

"No. But a group of men I remembered from the shakedown arrived around ten. I bussed their table, remaining silent and hopefully invisible."

He sips more coffee. "So one of the guys was staring at me. I remember him from the old days. Peter. A pretty stand-up guy as far as mobsters go. We hung out some when I was undercover. He never came right out and said it, but I think he only planned to stay in this line of work until he made enough money to clear out."

"That obviously didn't happen for him."

"No. I'm sure he made the money, but you just don't decide to clear out. And Peter knew everything. He was the upfront financial guy. Made everything come out on paper. Paid the right taxes. All that stuff."

"Like the Robert Duvall character in *The Godfather*."

"Yeah. In a way."

"So what happened?"

"I'll get to it. Don't worry. So anyway, on the way back to the hotel that night, I felt like somebody was following me. And sure enough it was true. But I didn't know who it was. I couldn't tell."

"Were you scared?"

"Spooked a little. It's been a while since I've been involved in that kind of thing. But not so long that I didn't know how to lose him."

"Oh good."

"Last night I went back. Worked until around ten thirty, and Peter corners me in the kitchen."

"Oh, no!"

"Yep. He pulls me out back and I'm thinking, *This is it. I am going to die.* He's not going to waste punches and threats. He'll just pop me right in the head."

"Dad!"

"Sorry. It's true."

"Well, obviously he didn't do that."

"No." He smiles and takes off his leather jacket. "So I asked him if there was a problem with my service. And he leaned forward and asked if I had a problem with them. I shook my head. 'I just want to find my wife. That's all. I don't know anything, only that I haven't seen her in fifteen years.'"

This is amazing.

"Peter said, 'Let's go for a drive,' and though all my training told me not to go, I knew it was okay. So we drove down to one of the docks near Domino Sugar. And he told me about Vince."

"Who's Vince?"

"One of the meanest thugs in the organization. But he had that sort of twisted honor some of them have. He would have never hurt anybody for his own sake. So here's the crux of the story."

"Should Charley hear this? She's out with Harris."

"I'll tell you first." He picks up his coffee mug, then sets it back down. "They kept Babette for several weeks. He said it was obvious Vince was falling in love with her, and one night, they both disappeared."

"You're kidding!"

He shakes his head.

"Why didn't they go after him?"

"They tried, but they couldn't find a trace. But Peter knew Vince pretty well. He really thought I was dead and figured Vince needed to get out. He told me Vince's grandmother lived in Jackman, Maine. He figured he took Babette up that way. It's so remote. He doubted they would have found him even if they had tried. Well, some of them did try, but only Peter knew about Maine."

"Wow. And that's pretty much it?"

"Yes. It isn't much, but it's a direction to go in, a lead to follow. And since we had no leads before yesterday, I find it encouraging."

"Me too."

"So"—he squeezes my hand—"I'm thinking a trip to Maine after this shoot is over might be a good idea."

"Me too, Dad. I mean, who knows what we'll find, or even if we'll find her at all. But we've got to try."

"I'd say you're exactly right."

I ask him if we can go to Appalachia while we're at it.

He raises his brows. "What for?"

"There are some people I think I should meet."

I tell him about Megan, the children's home, and everything that's been happening inside of me the past couple of days since I've been reading the gospels. "This Christian life is about so much more, Dad! I mean, I think it could be pretty exciting, don't you?"

"I do. We'll do it. I wonder if Charley would go with us. We can just take the RV."

"Oh, Dad. I think Charley will have plans of her own."

"So tell me all about it."

And I do.

2:45 p.m.

Angus: The band is doing great. And there's funnel cake.

Me: Wonderful!

Angus: We won't be leaving until tomorrow morning. Can I take you to dinner instead of coffee on Monday?

A real dinner date!

Me: Sounds like a plan.

Angus: I'll pick you up at 6:15.

Me: That's fine. I'll be ready.

Angus: Okay. See you tomorrow, Scotty.

Me: See you. Drive carefully!

Angus: Bye.

Monday, May 14, 8:30 a.m.

Angus's dad is standing outside the TrailMama's door. "Special delivery."

A large box sits in the back of his truck.

"My harp!"

"Is that what this is?"

"Yes!"

"Let me help you get it inside."

"Thanks!" I accompany him to the truck.

He sets the harp down inside the RV.

"What's that?" Dad asks.

"A Celtic harp."

"When did you order that?"

"Almost two weeks ago."

He shakes his head. "Only you, Scotty."

Ain't that the truth?

Mr. Matheson takes his leave, shoulders weary. And I wonder how soon the red cup will emerge? It's easy to be angry at him, but I feel sorry for him. He's destroyed his family and he knows it but seems powerless to stop what he's doing. How does a man just stop drinking?

Charley and Dad help me remove the harp from the box. Its carved wood glows with warmth and I run my fingers along the strings. "Whoa," I whisper. "Isn't that beautiful?"

"My goodness," Charley says.

"You're really going to learn to play this thing?" Dad. "'Cause I hope you do. I could stand to listen to this."

"Me too, baby." Charley. "It's so peaceful."

"Yeah," I say. Yeah. I can do this.

Each of us plucks the instrument a little bit, and I'm sure it must be out of tune after the shipping, but it doesn't matter.

"It will be nice having music around, won't it, George?" Charley says, sitting on the sofa.

"I can't think of anything nicer."

I love having a family. I really do.

11:00 a.m.

Charley storms inside the trailer. "That's it! I'm done. I've quit. I may never eat lunch in this town again, but you know what? I don't even care."

I bust out laughing about the lunch thing, then feel bad. She's entirely serious.

"What happened?" Dad asks.

"I've been yelled at, called names, and ridiculed for the last time, George. I don't have to take that."

He removes his glasses and shuts his laptop. "No, you sure don't. I'm proud of you."

"Me too!" I take her bag and set it on the sofa.

"So let's go. Let's just get out of here."

"What about Anthony Harris?" What about my date with Angus?

"He knows what happened. He says he understands and he'll meet up with us after the shoot, wherever that happens to be."

How 'bout Maine?

Still, I've got to salvage my date. "Don't you think it would make a stronger statement if you don't pull out right away? We've rented this space. Can we just stay one more night and pull out in the morning?" Oh man! My voice has a trill of desperation in it.

"Why?" she asks.

"Yeah, Scotty"—Dad rests his forearm on the table, a twinkle in his eye—"how come?"

I cross my arms over my chest. "Because I've got a date tonight. Okay? My first real dinner date. And I really want to go on it. Please?"

Tears mist up Charley's eyes. "Oh, baby!"

"Now don't go getting all misty on us," Dad says.

"I can't help it. Our baby. On her first date? Is it with the bagpiper?"

I nod.

She turns to Dad. "You're going to talk with him first, aren't you?"

Dad laughs. "That's a little old-fashioned, don't you think?"

"No. This is our Scotty. You've got to make sure nothing happens to her."

He nods. "I've got some tough shoes to fill, then."

"You do. She's worth it, though, George, you know how much, don't you?"

And the air settles with a heaviness because we're talking about so much more.

"I do. Scotty is everything to me."

Charley hugs me and heads into her cubicle.

This is the first step to good-bye.

2:45 p.m.

I finish up my final assignment for *Lady Oracle* and send it off to my teacher. "So what time do we ship out tomorrow morning?"

"Six," Dad says. "Before Maine, we're going to head up to see Grammie and Grampie for a couple of weeks. See the new place, get a tan, have your birthday."

"Nice. And we can help them move into the new place!"

"Grammie told me she'll be relying on you to help pick out furniture. She's afraid some of the stuff in storage will be ruined. Dad and I will head onto the storage unit and take care of that while you and Grammie have fun picking out colors."

"That sounds great." I close my laptop. Still can't blog. But I sent Violette the first round of the website and she loves it. All is well there.

Somebody knocks on the RV's door.

I hop down from my loft and open it. "Hi, Mr. Harris!"

"Scotty, dear."

"Tony!" Charley walks forward as he steps up into the TrailMama, and they embrace each other. She fits into him perfectly, her face even with his neck, her silver-blonde locks so beautiful with his gray hair. They pull back and look at each other and they are in love.

Thank you, God, she so deserves him.

"I'm proud of you for what you did with Evans." He squeezes her shoulder.

"I know, but I hate leaving."

He pulls out his pipe and just fiddles with it. "Are you heading to Delaware as expected, then?"

She nods. "It will be good for Scotty to spend time with her other grandparents."

"It's always good to be with family. I'll join you when the shoot's done"—he turns to my Dad—"if that's all right with you, Ezra." Then he winks. He knows. She's told him about our real life.

"The more the merrier, Anthony. We'd love to have you."

Imagine! Anthony Harris coming to Grammie and Grampie's house. Who would have ever seen this coming?

Harris is dressed in his military getup. "I'd better get back. But I'll come by in the morning before you take your leave. And Scotty, behave yourself on your date."

So Charley spilled the beans. "I will."

"Bagpipers canna always be trusted." He winks again. My goodness he's a winky one today. "I'll pick you up around seven tonight, dearie," he says to Charley.

"I'll be ready."

I follow him outside. "Mr. Harris, wait a sec."

"Certainly. I wanted to thank you for the good word you most certainly put in for me."

"Charley came to her own decision. I suppose she told you Jeremy bowed out."

"Aye. He's a good man for all of that. He knew what was best for your grandmother."

"You mean you?"

"Aye. I do love her, Scotty. I'll do what's best by her. I've been ready to settle back down for years. I was just waiting for the perfect woman to do it with."

"Perfect? I love my grandmother, but she's hardly perfect."

"Perfect for me."

"And there you'll get no argument from me."

He reaches out and I hug him, smelling pipe tobacco and toothpaste and wool.

"So will you ask her to marry you?"

"Eventually. Probably by the end of the summer. She realizes my faith is important to me. But she's coming around. I see that."

"Maybe she just needed to see God's got plans for her."

"Aye. Maybe she just needed someone to love her without her needing to do anything but be herself."

"That could be."

He leans forward and touches my nose. "In the meantime, Scotty dear, you and I will embark on a conspiracy of prayer for your grandmother. And we'll remember Saint Paul and how the Lord got hold of that rascal!" He booms a laugh.

"More difficult people than Charley have turned around."

"Aye, that's true enough."

"But what if she doesn't, Mr. Harris?"

"Oh, I've greater faith than that."

"Then I do too. Come see us as soon as the shoot's over."

"I promise you that."

He walks back down the dusty road toward the shoot. A lone Scotsman, kilt swinging, and his voice booms out, a beautiful baritone, singing "Amazing Grace."

Goosebumps rise on my arms and I realize that God sent Anthony Harris our way. Which shouldn't be surprising. God's got a way of sending his people to each other.

7:15 p.m.

Angus is looking good tonight. He wore his kilt, a white button-down shirt, and a dark green tie. We're sitting at Bouchon, an upscale French bistro. And we're eating escargot! This is so fun!

I dig a snail out of its shell and place the buttery, garlicky morsel on my tongue. It's amazing. I'm eating a snail for heaven's sake and it's amazing!

"Is your kilt the Matheson plaid?" Red, green, blue, and a fine light blue make up the pattern.

"Yes."

"It's really pretty. So how did your band do?"

"We came in first for bands, and I came in second for piping. It's really good at my age." He blushes. "I don't mean to be proud. I'm just excited."

"I think it's great." I grab a hunk of bread off the baguette between us and dip it in the butter and garlic around the escargot. I'm telling you, this is amazing. Who knew?

"I can't believe you're leaving tomorrow."

"Me either. It's weird how stuff happens so suddenly."

"No kidding." He breaks off a piece of bread.

"So, have you decided? About where to move to?"

"Yeah." He sighs. "I love it here in Asheville, but I've got to go with my mom. I mean, I'll be leaving for Scotland at the end of August and all."

"Why did you pick your mom?"

"I can't pick up the pieces for my father anymore. None of us can. My sister's already in Richmond. Left this morning."

"You're all moving in with that lady?"

He nods. "She's a college professor, does really well, and has a big old house. But there's a guest house too and we're taking that. Mom and Catriona will have to share a bedroom, but since she's got a year of college left, she won't be there much past summer."

"What's going to happen to your dad?"

The waiter tops off our water glass and asks how everything is. I tell him the escargot is, of course, amazing. All I can say is, I'm glad Angus is eating this much garlic too!

Angus takes a sip of water. "I honestly don't know what's going to happen to him. If he doesn't stop drinking, he'll probably lose the campground. If he was smart, he'd sell it right now before he runs it into the ground."

A bitter edge taints his voice, but I don't blame him. This is his father. This was the person who was supposed to show him how to be a man.

"But I can't make my dad's problems mine. Not when he's making his own choices. I found out from my aunt that mom's been threatening to leave him for years and he still didn't change his ways."

"Maybe he thought they were empty threats."

"Well, he hoped that, I'm sure. Anyway, I'm leaving for Richmond next week. Even the thought of this shoot, of staying around for the excitement isn't enough to keep me here." He clears his throat. "Can we talk about something else? I'd like to just have fun."

"You got it."

"I just finished reading *The Moon and Sixpence* by Somerset Maugham. The guy in the book was an even bigger jerk than . . . never mind. You read any Maugham yet?"

"No! Is he great?"

"Okay, after we eat we're headed to the bookstore."

When literary geeks go on a date.

Three hours later

The camp chapel is quiet and Angus and I sit holding hands. He has nice hands. Warm but not sweaty. And his fingers, used to playing the bagpipes I guess, aren't flimsy and wimpy. He actually *holds* my hand.

"So I'm taking it that we'll write and text and keep in touch that way?" he asks.

"Definitely. I'll want to hear how you're doing."

"Thanks."

I want to tell him I'll keep praying for him, but it's hard sometimes to offer up words like that. Sometimes prayers seem like a magic potion that's going to take away all the pain when really most times, they just help you get through it all.

"It's midnight." He squeezes my hand. "I'd better get back and see if Dad's okay."

"I understand. Will you be all right? Will he hurt you?"

Angus shakes his head. "No. Scotty, my Dad used to hit me a lot. When I was little. About three years ago, I landed a punch to his jaw and told him he'd better never hit me again."

"Oh my gosh."

"Yeah. I felt like I became a man that day. It was weird. I know you're not supposed to hit your father, but I'd had all I could take."

"It's okay. I can't say I wouldn't do the same thing." I mean, none of us can, unless we're in the situation.

"Can I kiss you good-bye? A real kiss?"

What a gentleman.

"Yes."

I turn toward him there on the pew and he turns toward me. He cradles my face in both of his hands and says, "You're so pretty, Scotty." And he leans forward and presses his lips against mine. I return the kiss, a sweet, wonderful kiss that we hold for just a couple of seconds.

He pulls back. "Thank you. For everything. I appreciate all you've done and been the past week or so."

"It wasn't really anything."

"Yeah, Scotty. It was."

He leans forward and gives me one more quick kiss before standing up. "I've gotta go. I don't want to."

"It's okay."

"Are you coming?"

"No. I think I'll sit here for a while. Should I lock up or something?"

"No. The door to the church is always open."

"That's just as it should be."

"You're right."

In the darkness, I watch him walk down the aisle, weighed down by sadness and the cares of all he's under. But when he opens the door, the street light silhouettes him and before it swings shut, I watch him jump down the steps, pump his fist in the air and say, "Yeah!" in a loud whisper.

So Lord, help Angus. Could you come down to him in ways you came to me that day in that church in Texas? Could you be the father he needs right now?

Some prayers you know God will answer.

Tuesday, May 15, 6:00 a.m.

"Scotty?"

I open my eyes. "Hey, Dad."

"We're about to set out. Two Scottish-looking guys want to say good-bye."

I jump down from the loft and throw on some sweats and a sweatshirt.

Angus and Harris stand by the picnic table.

We embrace each other in turn and I can't believe we're moving on so soon.

As we pull off the lot, I watch Harris turn to Angus and stick out his hand. The two shake and sit down at the picnic table together. Harris pulls out his pipe. I realize that God answered my prayer for Angus. And right quickly at that! As Harris might say.

Tuesday, June 6

Happy birthday to me! Seventeen years old today and feelin' groovy.

I'm sitting on the beach. The new house is furnished and Grammie let me pick out everything for my own room! Naturally I chose vintage modern. And when I couldn't get vintage, we found reproductions. My room is sleek and not at all befitting a teenager.

I'm just sayin'!

I set down my book. Yeah, I'm reading *The Great Gatsby* again. The sun shines warm on my face. Closing my eyes, I figure a little nap won't hurt a thing. I'm still doing school in a major way and will finish up early, but just today, I'm taking a break.

Major party planned by the fam tonight. And on Thursday we're headed up to Maine.

It feels so good in my beach chair.

The light behind my eyelids switches from blood-red to gray. The sun has gone away.

"You still haven't finished that book? Goodness gracious, girl, I thought you were a way faster reader than that!"

"Seth!" I scream, opening my eyes and jumping out of my chair. "What are you doing here?"

"Hey, I heard the hottest bash ever was happening right here this afternoon. I wouldn't miss something like that! Provided there are no red cups, of course."

I throw myself into his arms. Seth is here. I just can't believe it. "Who told you?"

"Dad. He said he and Mom were driving up, and it coincided with a break between films. I definitely didn't want to spend more time in LA. So here I am, crashing your party."

"Oh, crash away!" I squeeze him more tightly and we hold the embrace for a bit.

I pull away. "How was it, seeing your parents this time?"

"Perfect. Just right. Like it should have always been."

"Well, it may take you a while, but you learn eventually."

"With the bulldog Scotty Fitzgerald always yapping at my heels, it's hard not to get the message."

"You got that right, mister."

He plops down on the sand. I sit back down in my chair. "So how are you really doing?" I ask.

"Good. None of my old gang will have anything to do with me, due to Karissa. But that's a good thing. I've decided to do what you said. I'm going to buy a house around here, spend my off times out of LA, just make acting my job, not my whole life."

"Does that feel good?"

He smiles. "It really does."

"Nothing like that should consume us."

"And besides, since you've basically shut down your blog, I don't feel guilty about providing you fodder!" He laughs.

"You knew?"

"Yep."

"When?"

"In Marshall."

I feel heat rise to my face, and it's not a sunburn. "Oh, man."

"It's okay, Scotty. You were just working out a lot of things on that blog. I'm taking it you've learned some of your own lessons?"

I nod. "Like how much I don't need to be in the business of people I don't even know."

"You've got enough worries running the business of those you do!"

"Oh, Seth. I wish you weren't so right about that. But it's true."

"You love with a full heart, Scotty. And that's okay. Believe me, I don't know what I would have done without you."

5:00 p.m.

The cookout is in full swing! Everybody I think most highly of surrounds me. The cake is blazing with seventeen candles and here are the people who are singing:

Dad

Charley
Grammie
Grampie
Bob
Doris (they happened to be passing through)
Maisie (yes, I've finally met her in person!)
Edie
Steve
Seth
Harris
Ms. Burrelle, who flew in from Chicago
And, believe it or not . . .
Jeremy!

Yep. He came. And I'm so glad. No hard feelings between him and Charley. Friends to the end.

But one place is still empty around the cake table, and we're hoping against hope that soon it will be filled.

Tomorrow, Dad and I leave for Maine. We're taking the TrailMama, and Charley is heading to Scotland to check out Harris's farm and castle. "I promise we'll behave ourselves," he assured me when I said they'd better not do anything they'd regret.

The song ends, I blow out the candles, and everyone claps. I smile at all of them. My life is full and rich, and for this moment I believe that heaven has come to earth.

About the Author

LISA SAMSON is the author of twenty books, including the Christy Award-winning *Songbird.* Her young adult books also include *Hollywood Nobody* and *Finding Hollywood Nobody.* She speaks at various writers' conferences throughout the year. Lisa and her husband, Will, reside in Kentucky with their three children. Learn more about Lisa at www.lisasamson.com.